AROUND THE WORLD IN 11 DAYS

I0677871

**Deboshree Bhattacharjee** is a writer and content consultant with a soft spot for bringing stories to life. She has a Masters in Communications and specializes in creating engaging content across education, lifestyle and marketing. Previously, Deboshree worked as the editorial lead with FirstCry.com and a public affairs professional with Edelman. Her work has been published in several digital magazines and short story collections including *Kaleidoscope, When Women Speak Up and Jukebox by WritersMelon.*

Deboshree lives in Pune with her husband, son and their furry brown dog. Every morning, she wakes up with the northern lights in her eyes and chalks out travel plans. You can find Deboshree on her personal blog, *Of Paneer, Pulao and Pune.*

LEARNING
GEOGRAPHY
THE FUN WAY

AROUND THE WORLD IN 11 DAYS

# DEBOSHREE
# BHATTACHARJEE

RUPA

Published by
Rupa Publications India Pvt. Ltd 2019
7/16, Ansari Road, Daryaganj
New Delhi 110002

*Sales Centres:*
Allahabad Bengaluru Chennai
Hyderabad Jaipur Kathmandu
Kolkata Mumbai

While all efforts have been made to make the images of the maps accurate,
the publisher and the author are in no way liable for the correctness or
authenticity of the same. Any errors or omissions brought to our attention
will be remedied in future editions. The maps in this book are not to scale.

The views and opinions expressed in this book are the author's own and
the facts are as reported by her which have been verified to the extent
possible, and the publishers are not in any way liable for the same.

ISBN: 978-93-5333-559-5

First impression 2019

10 9 8 7 6 5 4 3 2 1

The moral right of the author has been asserted.

# CONTENTS

# INTRODUCTION

Have you ever looked at the sky at night? On clear nights when there are no clouds, you can see thousands of stars. Sometimes you can also see shiny specks that look like stars but are much brighter. These are called **planets**, and there are billions of planets in the universe. And yet, there exists only one planet that is confirmed to have life—our Earth, the third planet from the sun. As of November 2018, the Earth inhabits 7.7 billion people and about 8.7 million species of animals.

When you see the other seven planets of our solar system—Mercury, Venus, Mars, Jupiter, Saturn, Uranus and Neptune—you look at large astronomical bodies where no one can live. Scientists are still foraging for life on Mars, but till date, no alien has come to meet us from the beyond. What is so special about the Earth that makes it the only planet among billions to sustain animals, plants, insects, birds and human beings?

## WHAT MAKES THE EARTH SPECIAL?

- **We have water.** The Earth is the only known planet in the solar system to have water on its surface in the form of oceans, rivers and lakes. About 71 per cent of the Earth's surface is covered with water. Can you imagine how life would continue if we didn't have water?

- **We are at _just_ the right distance from the Sun.** The average temperature of our planet is around 14°C. Now, compare this with the average temperatures of Venus (400°C) and Mars (-60°C)! The Earth does have some extreme temperatures, but it is nowhere near as harsh as the other planets in the solar system. The highest recorded temperature on Earth is 70.7°C in Iran's Lut Desert while the lowest is -89.2°C recorded at the Soviet Vostok Station in Antarctica.
- **We have a bright and reassuring moon—our very own natural satellite.** When the moon revolves around the Earth, it stabilizes the Earth's orbit around the Sun. Do you know what would happen if we had no moon? The Earth's orbit around the Sun would wobble and shake, wreaking havoc on our climate and seasons.

Imagine that an alien from outer space comes to visit you at home one day. 'Would you like to go and live on another planet?' the alien asks. 'It is very Earth-like, and I promise you'll live!' If you go along with the alien, up and away in a gigantic spaceship, what do you think will happen?

Well, you might find a planet where you can breathe. But what you're very unlikely to see is a planet with geography as unique as ours. The total area of the Earth is about 510 million sq km, and no two landmasses are alike. Nowhere else have scientists found lakes and rivers that flow, with beautiful swans and colourful fishes. No mountain ranges exist outside the Earth where the peaks are capped with snow and the forested valleys abound in pretty flowers and delicious fruits. Our tall waterfalls with their gurgling sounds are unique to the entire solar system. From erupting volcanoes with their masses of lava to picturesque islands where people fish for a living, the Earth is the most topographically varied planet to ever be discovered.

Get ready to embark on one of the most thrilling rides you have ever taken—a speed ride across the whole world! In this book, we will take a dazzling tour through various continents and countries, dive into the deepest oceans and row down the gushing rivers, escape narrowly from erupting volcanoes, and come face-to-face with wildlife in the depths of the forests. By the end of the tour, you will not only fall deeper in love with this beautiful planet we live in, but also understand it like the back of your hand.

So, have you packed your bags yet?

# CONTINENTS OF THE WORLD

If you see the Earth from afar, you will see patches of brown interspersed with patches of blue. The Earth isn't one uniform, continuous stretch of land, but comprises several landmasses, sometimes connected by oceans. These landmasses are called **continents**. They are high enough to not be flooded by the water bodies surrounding them.

## WAS THE EARTH ALWAYS SPLIT UP INTO CONTINENTS?

When the Earth was formed more than 4.6 billion years ago, it looked nothing like it does today. Our planet was a massive ball of burning gases that continually escaped into outer space. As the Earth cooled, the gases came together to form the atmosphere. Water remained in a gaseous form until the Earth cooled down further and the water condensed into rain, giving birth to our oceans. When the first landmasses emerged, they were all joined together as one massive landmass. This supercontinent was called **Pangaea**.

But Pangaea was not to be. Underneath the Earth's surface, something called **plate tectonics** worked at full steam. The landmass was forever in motion, and slowly, Pangaea split up into two smaller landmasses called **Gondwana** and **Laurasia**.

*Pangaea*

As time went by, the landmasses divided further to create the continents we know today. But guess what? The landmasses haven't stopped moving! Their boundaries are constantly changing, and you never know, they may even come together again or split up further in the future. Now you see why it is dangerous to stand on the edge of a cliff!

## THE SEVEN CONTINENTS

The present-day Earth is divided into **seven** continents: North America, South America, Antarctica, Europe, Asia, Africa and Australia. All of them have their unique climate, wildlife, vegetation, culture and lifestyle.

*The seven continents*

Have you fastened your seatbelts? Let's start our ride from the smallest continent on Earth. Look carefully, and you should be able to see a kangaroo hopping about with a little joey in her pouch...

## AUSTRALIA

Welcome to the smallest continent in the world!

Think 'Australia,' and a majority of the world conjures up images of kangaroos, a fiercely burning sun, the competitive Aussie cricket team and beautiful beaches. While the island country of Australia occupies the largest area in the continent of Australia, it is not the only country in this land Down Under. The Australian continent also comprises two other countries: Papua New Guinea and New Zealand, though the number of countries in Australia is a highly debated subject.

Sydney, one of the main cities in the country of Australia, is also the most populated, followed by Melbourne, Brisbane and Perth. From above, you can see that Australia is surrounded by two major water bodies: the Indian Ocean and the Pacific Ocean.

Australia is a progressive continent, with one of the most stable economies in the world. Many people in Australia are involved in the trade of minerals like iron ore, coal, wheat and processed metals. From hummock grasslands and shrubs in desert areas to tropical rainforests, different kinds of vegetation cover the continent.

## Dressing for the Weather

Now that you are in Australia, what should you wear to be comfortable? The average temperature of Australia is around 30°C in the summer and 15°C in the winter. Australian summers coincide with winter months in the Northern Hemisphere. However, the continent of Australia is divided into different climate zones:

**Northern Australia:** It is quite hot here during both the summer and winter seasons. While the summers are humid, the winters tend to be dry. Pack light cotton clothing with raincoats for summers, and slightly warmer clothes for winters.

**Southern Australia:** It is cooler here in both the seasons. Sometimes it rains during winters.

**Southeast Australia:** This is the region of the Tasmanian Mountains and the Australian Alps. It is cold throughout the year; so make sure to pack your sweaters and jackets.

**Central Australia:** This region has dry sweltering desert-like areas. Pack your most comfortable and lightweight clothes.

## Let's Go Sightseeing

Come on! Let's explore this rich continent packed with beautiful and unique sights. Have a sumptuous breakfast of eggs, grilled tomato, mushrooms and hash browns by the beaches of Melbourne or Gold Coast.

Enjoy an opera performance in the Sydney Opera House designed by Jørn Utzon, a Danish architect, in 1973. If you think it looks like a lotus, well, this is the building that inspired the famous Lotus Temple in New Delhi, India. Immerse yourself in the eucalyptus forests of the Blue Mountains, about 50 km away from Sydney. Walk along the Sydney Harbour Bridge—an architectural wonder that opened in 1932.

Drive past The Twelve Apostles—a group of stunning limestone stacks—in Victoria. They look grand, but also a little forbidding.

Deep down in the seas of Australia are 1,700 species of corals. The continent has the world's largest coral reef system called the Great Barrier Reef. Dive into the waters of the reef, located off the coast of Queensland, and get enchanted with corals of dazzling colours you did not know existed.

## Where the Wild Things Are

Look up at that eucalyptus tree! Do you see an inquisitive koala resting amidst the branches? Perhaps he is waiting for his jumping friends that just scampered behind the rocks—the kangaroos and the wallabies.

Wherever you look around in Australia, you can behold

beautiful flora and fauna, 80 per cent of which you won't find anywhere else in the world. The continent is home to the dingo—a large carnivorous dog. Hopping away to glory are the kangaroos and their smaller cousins, the wallabies. Koalas nestle among trees, frowning each time someone calls them a bear! (Koalas are not bears, but marsupials. Like kangaroos, a female koala carries her baby in her pouch until the little one can fend for itself.) Look down, and you'll find the wombat—a cuddly, burrowing animal that can give any teddy bear a run for its money.

Apart from marsupials, Australia is also home to the monotremes—mammals that lay eggs! Sounds strange, doesn't it? Well, the platypus and the echidna are Australian monotremes that lay eggs, but also feed their little ones on milk.

Australia is also home to 828 species of birds, half of which aren't found anywhere else. There is the flightless emu, the fancy-blue cassowary, the black currawong and the noisy kookaburra. Don't be scared if you think you heard a human being laughing hysterically in the wilderness. It will only be the kookaburra, whose call sounds almost exactly like that of a human being!

Beware of the funnel-web spider, also native to Australia. It can kill you within fifteen minutes of receiving the bite!

## EUROPE

Crystal clear blue skies, splendid palaces, grand castles and diverse foods—welcome to Europe! A trip to Europe is on the bucket list of most travellers, as the continent is home to some of the most beautiful countries, monuments and cultures.

Europe is bordered by the Arctic Ocean, the Atlantic Ocean, the Mediterranean Sea and the Black Sea. It also has several fascinating landforms, including the Alps and the Pyrenees—two of the largest mountain ranges in the world. Deciduous and coniferous trees like oak, maple, pine and fir cover large areas of Europe. As you climb up the mountains, you see lichens, shrubs and pretty little wildflowers.

The European continent is divided into fifty countries. Russia is the largest country in Europe while Vatican City—the home of the Pope—is the smallest. Some of the important countries in Europe for travel include Germany, France, Sweden and Spain.

## Wait—Since When is Russia a Part of Europe?

Russia has land in both Europe (23 per cent) and Asia (77 per cent). Even though most of its land is in Asia, 75 per cent of its people live in Europe. The Ural Mountains mark the border between Asia and Europe.

The European continent has long been the home of cultural and social evolution. It was here that the ancient Greek and Roman civilizations—the roots of most of our modern learning—flourished. The European Union (EU)—a political group of twenty-eight member states in Europe—is an influential organization in world politics.

## Dressing for the Weather

A pair of shoes isn't going to be enough when you're in Europe. You will need comfortable light footwear when you are in Spain, but thick winter boots will be mandatory during winters in Austria! During your European expedition, you will travel through multiple climate zones:

**Western Europe** (Austria, Netherlands, Germany): This is a very pleasant zone. You will find both the summers and winters mild here. There may be high humidity with considerable rain in some parts of the region.

**Northern Europe** (Norway, Finland, Sweden): It's going to be extremely cold here! There are snowstorms in the winters. Summers are milder and bring in some sunlight, for a short duration.

**Central and Eastern Europe** (Croatia, Hungary): This area experiences a cool summer humid continental climate. But don't discount snowfall during winters!

**Mountain zones** (Swiss Alps): No surprises here—you are going to feel cold, all night and day! Glaciers and snow cover everything throughout the year.

**Mediterranean region** (Italy, Greece): This place is bliss on Earth! The summers are sunny, the winters are fairly mild, and you get a comfortable spring and autumn.

## Let's Go Sightseeing

From drinking coffee at a quaint café in Prague to climbing to the top of the Eiffel Tower in Paris or visiting the ancient ruins in Rome to sunbathing in Croatia, your European tour is multifaceted and wonderful.

Visit the Anne Frank House in Amsterdam and visualize how the little Anne hid there during the Holocaust at the time of World War II, holding on to dear life.

Get inside the structure of an atom at the Atomium in Brussels. This 102-metre-tall metal structure of an atom will make all those science classes super easy!

Take a rollercoaster ride at the Tivoli Gardens in Copenhagen, one of the oldest amusement parks in the world. It opened in 1843!

Enjoy some of the world's most famous paintings and sculptures displayed at the Louvre Museum in France. It is the world's largest art museum. Guess who sits here waiting for you! That's right, Mona Lisa, the damsel with the enigmatic smile!

Be awestruck at the Rialto Bridge in Venice, Italy, as you ride in one of the famous gondolas, a traditional Venetian boat.

Travel back in time to ancient Greece at the Parthenon, an old temple at the Acropolis in Athens. It is a temple dedicated to the Goddess Athena, the goddess of wisdom and war. Seems strange to worship both wisdom and war, doesn't it?

Get mesmerized by the Northern Lights in Iceland, also called the aurora borealis. This electrical phenomenon creates a dazzling display of colours in the night sky.

Check the time at the Big Ben in London, one of the most prominent symbols of the United Kingdom (UK). The great hour bell weighs 15.1 tons. It leans slightly (about 0.04 degrees) under all that weight. This is still a long way behind the famous Leaning Tower of Pisa in Italy that leans at about 3.99 degrees.

## But I Thought the UK Wasn't in Europe Anymore!

You may have heard that the UK is planning 'on leaving Europe'. Does that mean it is no longer part of the European continent? Well, it is, and always will be. The UK is planning to leave the

EU, which is a political group of twenty-eight member states. All the members of the EU follow a standard set of laws. People can move about freely across these nations and participate in trade. If Britain exits from the EU, it will cease to belong to this political and economic group. However, because of its geographical location, it will still be a part of the continent of Europe. As of June 2019, Brexit is still pending.

## Where the Wild Things Are

In the lowland forests of Europe, you will find the Eurasian wolf—a huge predator like the big bad wolf you must have read about in *Little Red Riding Hood*. Giving him fearsome company is the Eurasian brown bear. Despite its large size, this bear eats a rather tame meal of plants, insects and small mammals.

What's that near your feet? The European viper, also known as the common adder, is a poisonous snake species commonly found in Europe.

Flying in the European skies are several species of birds. Watch out for the Spanish imperial eagle—an endangered bird of prey. Thanks to conservation efforts, the population of this majestic bird has recovered to some extent.

## ANTARCTICA

If you have tucked your scarves and jackets in the recesses of your bag, bring them out at once! We are now onwards to the southernmost and coldest continent of the world—Antarctica.

Look at the large glaciers and huge sheets of white around you. Hardly a soul is in sight, for Antarctica is one of the most uninhabitable and least populated places on Earth. Did you know that there are zero countries in Antarctica? About 4,000 people live at the science stations. What a hard life they must lead!

## Dressing for the Weather

Throughout the year, Antarctica is severely cold. In the summer, the temperature ranges from -5°C to -20°C. In the winter, the temperature averages at -49°C! Antarctica also sees violent snowstorms that can leave you stunned and directionless. You have to wear special expedition clothing that includes several layers of clothes, thermal underwear and waterproof jackets.

## Let's Go Sightseeing

If you thought no one could visit Antarctica, prepare to be surprised. Although Antarctica is very remote, many voyages now let adventurous travellers explore this lonely continent.

Enjoy spectacular glaciers, icebergs and snowscapes, and watch the sun rise on a shimmering wintry world.

Meet penguins and seals in their natural habitat. Enjoy sea kayaking with humpback whales. Visit Ukraine's Vernadsky Research Station, the centre where scientists discovered a hole in our ozone layer.

Climb up Mount Vinson, one of the seven summits of the world (the highest peaks of each of the seven continents). Mount Vinson, at 4,897 m, is the tallest peak in Antarctica. If you are feeling particularly adventurous, trek right upto the South Pole. Don't even dream of doing this without preparation, or you might never return!

## Where the Wild Things Are

How can anyone survive in such cold climates? Well, human beings may find it tough, but many species of plants and animals manage just fine. In little nooks and crannies, you will discover algae, mosses, lichens, fungi and liverworts. These plants are specially adapted to survive extreme temperatures and dehydration. You won't find any trees or shrubs in Antartica. As for flowers, consider yourself lucky if you come across one of the only two flowering plant species in this continent: the Antarctic hair grass and the Antarctic pearlwort.

The cutest animals living in Antarctica are the seals. Seals are excellent swimmers that survive on fish, squid and crustaceans. Antarctica has as many as six different species of seals. Weddell seals can grow up to be as heavy as 400 kg! It is a miracle that they can swim with all that body weight!

Look, who's that walking up to you with two babies? The penguins are native to Antarctica and are adorable with their human-like gait and lovely black-and-white coat. The common species of penguins you will find in Antarctica are the Adélie penguins, the emperor penguins, and the chinstrap penguins. The male penguins remain very busy and do most of the child-rearing work. A male Adélie penguin incubates the eggs for thirty-five days—going without food for all that time—while the mother returns to the sea to feed. Now that's what you call shared parenting!

Antarctica is also home to many species of whales including toothed whales and baleen whales. The blue whale—the largest animal on Earth—also lives in Antarctica. They can be 24–30 m long with a weight of 1,40,000 kg! Don't worry, though; the whales in Antarctica are not known to attack human beings.

## SOUTH AMERICA

Hope you didn't get frostbitten in the icy climes of Antarctica! Our expedition has now arrived in South America—the fourth smallest continent of the world, with weather that's a good deal warmer and comfier than you experienced down south.

South America is bordered by the Atlantic and Pacific oceans. This continent is rich with beautiful geographical structures. Although the Nile is traditionally considered the longest river, some scientists claim it is the Amazon. It is also home to the Angel Falls, the world's highest waterfall with a height of 979 m, and the Mount Aconcagua, the world's tallest mountain outside Asia. While Aconcagua has a height of 6,958 m, Mount Everest stands at 8,848 m. All of us must look tinier than ants from up there!

The South American continent is divided into twelve countries. Brazil is the largest, followed by Colombia, Argentina and Peru.

### Dressing for the Weather

Bring out all your light, warm-weather clothes, for you are going to need a lot of those during your South American tryst. The continent experiences mostly mild to warm climate. The hottest and coldest temperatures ever recorded here were 48.9°C and -32°C, both recorded in Argentina. Broadly, the continent is divided into the following climate zones:

**Tropical—Wet or Dry:** The Amazon basin experiences this type of very hot and wet climate. Colombia is particularly wet, and has been experiencing 354 inches of precipitation annually. Doesn't sound too comfortable, eh? Some areas in South America experience a dry tropical climate where it is quite hot but not rainy.

**Mediterranean:** If you go to the Chilean Central Valley, you will find warm temperatures all through the year, with more rainfall in autumn and winter.

**Arid/Desert:** Some areas of the continent like Northern Chile see high temperatures with very little rainfall.

**Alpine:** High up in the Andes, it is cold throughout the year. Hence the population in these areas is low.

## Let's Go Sightseeing

Where should we start? At the beautiful Angel Falls in Venezuela or the Moai statues on Easter Island in Chile? South America is full of awe-inspiring sights, so hold your breath.

Travel to a surreal world in Machu Picchu, built by the Inca Empire between 1450 and 1460. It is a stone citadel high up in the mountains at 2,430 m. The stones were fitted without any mortar. But if you were to use a knife and try to crack a stone, you would fail. Our advice would be—don't try it! Machu Pichhu, or the Old Mountain, is a UNESCO World Heritage Centre. It is up to us to preserve the cultural heritage of the world.

Sit on a swing at Banos in Ecuador and travel right to the end of the world. This swing is located at a height of

2,600 m above sea level. From the swing, you can observe Mount Tungurahua, an active volcano. The cliff is as close to the 'end' as anyone would like to get!

Explore the Atacama Desert in Chile, and see stunning arid landscapes. Or walk through the Amazon rainforest, the largest rainforest in the world. Many sections of this forest are still unknown, and home to many secrets.

## Where the Wild Things Are

In a continent so densely forested and with such biodiversity, our wild friends are sure to abound. In the deepest corners of the forest lies the anaconda, the world's largest snake that can grow up to about 9 m and weigh 250 kg!

In the jungle, there prowls the grand jaguar—the third biggest cat after lions and tigers. The jaguar is also a symbol of speed and power. Have you seen a Jaguar car? It is a luxury automobile brand owned by the British company Jaguar Land Rover.

Both the jaguar and the anaconda love feeding on the capybara—a large rodent that struts around the South American jungles.

South America is also home to the sloth. If the jaguar stands for energy and grace, the sloth stands for its exact opposite. It has developed a reputation as one of the laziest animals ever to live! Can you imagine why? Well, some sloths are known to sleep for 15–18 hours a day!

Another unique animal in South America is the tapir. It looks a bit like a pig but is also related to horses and rhinos. It has an extra-long nose. The tapir doesn't poke its nose in other people's affairs; it uses its nose to grab fruits and leaves!

## NORTH AMERICA

Hey, another America! Is this continent connected to South America in any way? Well, some geologists believe that millions of years ago, a great ocean flowed between North America and South America. With time, the ocean receded and what we now have left is a narrow strip of land called the Isthmus of Panama. It lies between the Caribbean Sea and the Pacific Ocean. The Isthmus of Panama is believed to have been formed about 2.8 million years ago. Let's cross the canal to travel to North America, the third largest continent in the world.

Surrounding North America are the Atlantic Ocean, the Pacific Ocean, the Arctic Ocean and the Panama Canal. It is a continent with an incredibly interesting geographical terrain. Check out the Great Plains, a grassland that lies west of the Mississippi, the longest river in North America. Be awed by the tall peaks of the Rocky Mountains. Go from the top of Mount McKinley in Alaska (6,194 m above sea level) to the depths of the Death Valley in California (86 m below sea level). Temperatures in the Death Valley can reach 56.6°C, and yes, people die of the heat.

North America is divided into twenty-three countries, of which Canada is the largest by area. Mexico City, the capital of Mexico, is the most populated city in North America. The United States of America (US), considered one of the most powerful nations in the world, is also part of North America.

## Dressing for the Weather

Let's just say, you better pack multiple suitcases with clothes for vastly different kinds of weather. North America has many climate zones with amazing variation.

**Desert:** Be prepared for extreme temperatures with hardly any rain. The Death Valley is known for its desert climate.

**Grassland:** Here you will find hot summers and cold winters. Rainfall is usually ample.

**Mediterranean:** Temperatures are mostly warm all through the year. It rains during autumn and winter.

**Mountain:** It's freezing here! While winters can be below-freezing, things are a tad warmer in the short summers.

**Rainforest:** These areas are very hot and wet.

## Bad Weather Alert!

North America is infamous for its extreme weather phenomena, including tornadoes, hurricanes and thunderstorms. There is an area in the United States called the **Tornado Alley**. It gets up to 1,250 tornadoes every year! Geologists believe that the United States sees so many tornadoes because of its proximity to the Rocky Mountains and the Gulf of Mexico. These geographical structures create horizontal winds that intensify with height.

## Let's Go Sightseeing

Brace up, for it's going to be a fun-filled, adventurous ride! North America is chock-a-block with historical and geographical wonders. Here you will find the magical world of Walt Disney that has captivated millions of people since it first opened in Anaheim, California in 1955.

Let the Niagara Falls soak you and fill your ears with a

thunderous noise. These falls are located on the border of the United States and Canada.

Be amazed seeing the geysers at Yellowstone National Park, located in Wyoming, Montana. These geysers erupt and throw up hot water from deep within the Earth. The Steamboat Geyser in this park is the world's tallest active geyser. It has produced eruptions up to 122 m in height!

Tour the Grand Canyon on the Colorado River basin. It is 1,857 m deep; so be careful not to trip over!

Click pictures at the Statue of Liberty located on Liberty Island in New York City. It is 93 m tall. But did you know that this famous statue was actually a gift? It was dedicated by the people of France to the United States. A French civil engineer, Gustave Eiffel, built it and dedicated it to the United States in 1886.

## Where the Wild Things Are

Don't let the razzmatazz of Times Square in New York fool you! The North American continent is home to many wild creatures that live in the forests, away from the glitz and glamour. You have to be wary of the Arizona bark scorpion that likes to live in packs. Its venom can be dangerous even to human beings.

Another deadly animal you might meet in North America is the American alligator. It usually eats small animals, but it doesn't mind biting into a human being now and then!

## Alligators Are Not Crocodiles

Alligators usually have a U-shaped nose, unlike crocodiles that have a V-shaped one. Dare to look closer? You will see some portions of a crocodile's teeth visible even when it closes its jaws. But an alligator's teeth get completely hidden.

North America is also home to cute little raccoons. They can even come up to your backyard! But as friendly as baby raccoons may seem, remember that wild animals can easily feel threatened and get aggressive if they are afraid.

Somewhere in the North American jungles are jaguars and mountain lions. Do you know that mountain lions have many names? Cougar, puma and panther all refer to the same animal.

## AFRICA

Our tour across the world has now brought us to the second largest continent on Earth—Africa. Doesn't thinking about Africa instantly get you excited about wildlife safaris? From amazing flora and fauna to some of the most interesting food on the planet, the continent of Africa is waiting to be explored. If you were to come here from Europe, you could arrive in no time at all. The two continents are only 14.3 km apart at the Strait of Gibraltar!

Surrounding Africa are the Indian Ocean, the Atlantic Ocean, the Mediterranean Sea and the Red Sea. The Nile runs along Africa. It is the longest river in the world.

The African continent is comprised of fifty-four countries, the largest being Algeria, followed by the Democratic Republic of the Congo and Sudan. Lagos in Nigeria is the largest city in Africa.

## Dressing for the Weather

'If you're going to Africa, you should pack your best summer clothes!' Did someone say that to you before the expedition? It is true that many areas of Africa have hot climates. The hottest temperature ever recorded there was 57.8°C, in Libya. But did you know it snows in the Atlas Mountains of Africa? During your African sojourn, you will find the following climate zones:

**Tropical:** The central part of Africa sees high temperatures with heavy rainfall.

**Desert:** Many regions of Africa, such as the Sahara Desert, experience extreme heat with long dry spells. The Kalahari Desert in the southern part of Africa gets some rain during summer.

**Mediterranean:** The areas to the north and south of the desert see hot summers and cooler, wetter winters.

## Let's Go Sightseeing

Africa is an amazing continent to visit. Before you buckle your seat belt in your jungle jeep, make sure you visit the Victoria Falls in Zambia. These waterfalls are also called Mosi-oa-Tunya or the 'The Cloud That Thunders'. They are 108 m high!

Get lost amidst the grand Pyramids of Giza in Egypt. The early Egyptians constructed these magnificent monuments as tombs for their dead. They believed in an afterlife and often stuffed the tombs with the favourite objects of the deceased.

While in Egypt, also check out the Sphinx—the 19.8-metre tall statue of a lion with a human head. It stands for the combination of a lion's strength and a king's intelligence.

Cruise down the Nile and visit the Valley of the Kings. Here you'll find rock tombs of the pharaohs or ancient kings.

## Where the Wild Things Are

Ah, you are finally on the safari of a lifetime! Watch out for the majestic African lion as it lazes about in the sun with its family. The lion is a vulnerable species whose population is seriously going down due to human activity.

Look, who are those massive creatures crossing the riverbank? The African elephants! These elephants can weigh up to 6,000 kg. But for all their weight, they are herbivorous.

Hiding behind those dense canopies is the leopard—an excellent predator. Don't be fooled by its sleek body; it can kill prey up to three times its weight.

You'll also spot the giraffes munching steadily on grass in the daylight. Their necks are so long that they have special veins to help them bend over and drink water without losing consciousness!

In the waters of the Nile lives the African crocodile. It is the largest living reptile and can reach up to 6 m in length!

Africa is also renowned for its zebras with their unique black-and-white markings, along with hippos, rhinos and buffalos.

## ASIA

Welcome to the last leg of your cross-continental tour! You are now in Asia—the largest continent on Earth by both area and population. Asia is surrounded by the Pacific Ocean, the Indian Ocean and the Arctic Ocean. Asia is home to some of the oldest civilizations of the world, including the Indus Valley Civilization or the Harappan Civilization. Modern-day Asia is a hotbed of many cultures. You can listen to bells tolling merrily in the Hindu temples of India, or join the Buddhists as they chant every evening. Asia has become an important centre of trade and manufacturing and is key to the world economy.

The Asian continent is divided into forty-eight countries. The largest of these in area is Russia, followed by China and India. Asian geography is varied and stunning. There are mountain ranges as majestic as the Himalayas and plateaus as high as the Tibetan Plateau (4,877 m). It also has Lake Baikal in Russia, the deepest lake in the world at 1,620 m.

## Dressing for the Weather

Here's to hoping you kept both your summer and winter clothes clean! Most of Asia enjoys a continental climate which involves an extreme annual range—hot summers and cold winters. However, there are several climatic zones across the continent:

**Temperate:** These areas experience warm and wet summers while the winters are dry and bitter. You'll find this climate in Korea, Japan and China.

**Tropical:** The range of temperature is smaller here. While summers are wet, it can also rain in the winters. Areas in Myanmar, Thailand and India experience this climate.

**Mediterranean:** This region is quite mild, with cool weather in the summer that drops further in the winter. Cyclones are common in the winter and usually bring rain. Syria, Israel and Iraq fall in this climate zone.

## Let's Go Sightseeing

A trip through Asia promises to offer one thing—excitement at each moment! From the glorious beaches of Sri Lanka to the delicious noodles in China, the Taj Mahal in India to the cherry blossoms in Japan, there is never a dull moment as you explore the Asian continent.

Take a purifying bath in the Ganges at Varanasi in India. The waters of this river are considered to have holy powers.

Climb up to the Tiger's Nest in Bhutan—located 3,109 m above the Paro Valley. But don't expect to see a tiger there. The name comes from the legend of Guru Rinpoche, a Buddhist master from the eighth century, who allegedly flew there on the back of a tiger.

Visit the Lost City of Angkor Wat in Cambodia. It was the capital city of the Khmer Empire back in 1010-1220.

Experience the ambience of Changi Airport in Singapore. What's so special about this airport? Only the fact that it is considered the world's best, and has everything from a gym and a swimming pool to a movie theatre and a butterfly garden!

Walk along the Great Wall of China. Well, the whole wall stretches upto 21,196 km, so you're unlikely to have the energy to walk it all! Did you know that even though the wall is so large, it cannot really be seen from space?

## Where the Wild Things Are

You might have heard of the Asiatic lions and elephants, and of course, the monkeys. But Asian wildlife is much more diverse than that. Behold the grand Bengal tiger that lives in India. It is India's national animal. Sadly, the Bengal tiger is a vulnerable species whose population is on the decline due to human activity.

The Bactrian camel, with its two humps, is also a sight to behold. It lives in the deserts of Mongolia. Its two humps store enough water to help it survive the extreme weather.

A deadly creature that might cross your path in Asia is the king cobra. It lives primarily in the Middle East, India and China. The poison it injects in one bite can kill twenty people!

The cutest animal in Asia has got to be the giant panda. Native to China, the furry panda eats bamboo leaves and shoots.

## EXERCISE 1: HIGHLIGHTS FROM YOUR INTERCONTINENTAL TRIP

Welcome back to the base station! Study the maps below and identify the continent:

1.

This massive continent doesn't exist anymore! Name it.

_____

2.

Look carefully, and you'll see three big mountain ranges in this continent—the Pyrenees, the Alps and the Ural Mountains. Name it._____

3

Beware! The Tornado Alley in this continent might catch you! Where are you? _____

4.

We're in the continent of the Great Barrier Reef—the most stunning coral reef in the world you'll ever see. Where are we?

_____

5.

Enjoy some piri piri sauce as you write down the name of the continent shown on the map above. _____

6.

Macchu — Pichu

High up in the mountains here is the mysterious citadel of Machu Picchu. Which continent is this?_____

7.

Hundreds of years ago, the Indus Valley Civilization flourished in this continent. Name it._____

# COUNTRIES OF THE WORLD

Bet your trip across the seven continents of the Earth left you asking for more! Did you notice that every continent had different kinds of settlements—cities, villages, jungles, etc.? Continents are so huge in area that it is almost impossible for anyone to look after them in its entirety. For administrative and political purposes, continents are divided into smaller landmasses called **countries**. Every country in the world has a defined border that separates it from other countries.

As of March 2019, the total number of countries in the world is **195**. While the Australian continent has only three countries, Africa has fifty-four! All countries have their own capital cities from where the government functions.

Let us start the next phase of our journey—a sneak peek into the major countries of the world.

## THE COUNTRIES IN AUSTRALIA

Australia, the smallest continent on Earth, is divided into only three countries: Australia, New Zealand and Papua New Guinea. But you may be told that Australia actually has fourteen countries. Isn't this confusing?

The continent of Australia is part of a larger geographical structure called Oceania. Oceania includes many small island countries in the Pacific Ocean. The total number of countries in Oceania is fourteen, including Australia. But then, why isn't Oceania considered the main continent instead of Australia? It is because Oceania is not a *continuous* landmass. It includes scattered islands and coral atolls. Nauru, the smallest country in Oceania, has an area of only 21 sq km.

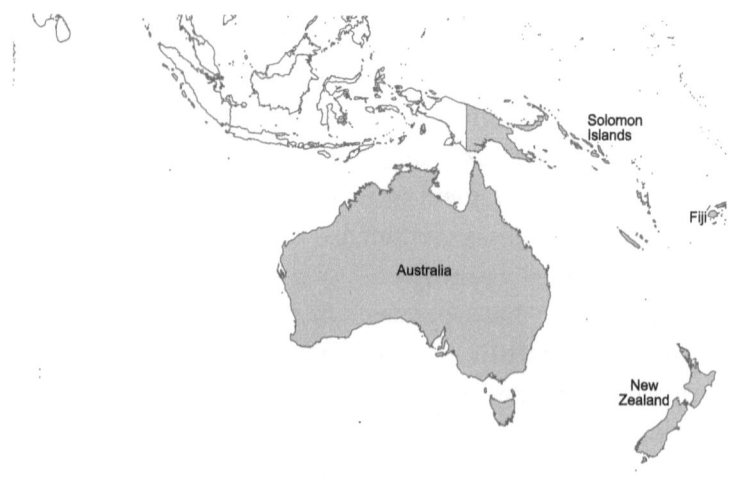

## LIST OF COUNTRIES IN OCEANIA
*(from largest to smallest by area)*

| COUNTRY | CAPITAL |
| --- | --- |
| Australia | Canberra |
| Papua New Guinea | Port Moresby |
| New Zealand | Wellington |
| Solomon Islands | Honiara |
| Fiji | Suva |
| Vanuatu | Port Vila |
| Samoa | Apia |
| Kiribati | South Tarawa |

| Tonga | Nuku´alofa |
| --- | --- |
| Federated States of Micronesia | Palikir |
| Palau | Ngerulmud |
| Marshall Islands | Majuro |
| Tuvalu | Funafuti |
| Nauru | Yaren |

## AUSTRALIA

The land you will now explore was first trodden by the aboriginal people—the early inhabitants of Australia who came from the Torres Strait Islands. Today, Australia is a thriving, developed country with 22.9 million people. The primary language is English. More than 50 per cent of the population practise Christianity. The official currency is the Australian dollar.

**Capital City:** Canberra is the capital of Australia, but Sydney and Melbourne are much bigger cities. Can you guess why Canberra was chosen? It seems Sydney and Melbourne couldn't stop arguing among themselves!

**Must-see in Australia:** Don't miss out on the Great Barrier Reef. It is a 2300 km-long ecosystem, the largest in the world. You'll not see such stunning corals anywhere else!

While in Australia, enjoy your time under the sun. The country has sunny weather, plenty of beaches and people who love energetic sports like surfing and cricket. The Australian national cricket team has won the World Cup five times till date!

## NEW ZEALAND

Let's go to the south of Australia and land in the beautiful country of New Zealand. Never make the error of assuming that New Zealand is part of the country of Australia! It has been independent since the nineteenth century, before which it was part of the British Crown. It is a developed country with over 4.7 million people, many of whom speak English, followed by Māori. More than 40 per cent of the people are Christians. The official currency is the New Zealand dollar.

**Capital City:** The current capital is Wellington. It is smaller than the largest city of Auckland, which is also the former capital. The first capital of New Zealand was Old Russell.

**Must-see in New Zealand:** Check out Wai-O-Tapu—a natural geothermal wonderland with bubbling mud, colourful springs and volcanic craters. You'll feel as if you've walked right into a sinister story.

Enjoy your time with the Kiwis. They are known to be hardworking yet fun-loving—just the perfect balance, don't you think?

## FIJI

It always seems to be holiday time in this stunning coastal country of around nine lakh people. It is one of the most popular holiday destinations in the world, and home to people of multiple ethnicities including those of Indian, Chinese and European descent. You will find churches, temples and mosques. Most people speak Fijian, Fiji Hindi or English. The Fijian dollar is the national currency.

**Capital City:** Suva is the capital of Fiji and also the centre of economic activity in this middle-income country. Before Suva, Levuka was the capital of Fiji.

**Must-see in Fiji:** Bathe in the Tavoro Waterfalls located in Fiji's Taveuni Island. This island is called Fiji's 'Garden of Eden' because it has amazing orchids and ferns that don't seem to belong to this era, but to a prehistoric world.

Have a wonderful time in Fiji with its rustling palm trees, sunny days and turquoise seas.

## THE COUNTRIES IN EUROPE

After your tour through the smallest continent, let's travel again to Europe. The European continent has as many as fifty countries! Of these fifty, some countries have territories in both Europe and Asia. These include Russia, Turkey, Georgia, Azerbaijan and Kazakhstan.

Countries keep getting added to Europe as smaller nations declare their independence. The latest country to become part of Europe is Kosovo, which became independent from Serbia in 2008. As of 2018, it is the second youngest country in the world after South Sudan in Africa, which separated from Sudan in 2011.

# LIST OF COUNTRIES IN EUROPE
*(from largest to smallest by area)*

| COUNTRY | CAPITAL |
|---------|---------|
| Russia | Moscow |
| Ukraine | Kiev |
| France | Paris |
| Spain | Madrid |
| Sweden | Stockholm |
| Norway | Oslo |
| Germany | Berlin |
| Finland | Helsinki |
| Poland | Warsaw |
| Italy | Rome |
| United Kingdom | London |
| Romania | Bucharest |
| Belarus | Minsk |
| Kazakhstan | Astana |
| Greece | Athens |
| Bulgaria | Sofia |
| Iceland | Reykjavik |
| Hungary | Budapest |
| Portugal | Lisbon |
| Austria | Vienna |
| Czech Republic | Prague |
| Serbia | Belgrade |
| Ireland | Dublin |

| | |
|---|---|
| Lithuania | Vilnius |
| Latvia | Riga |
| Croatia | Zagreb |
| Bosnia and Herzegovina | Sarajevo |
| Slovakia | Bratislava |
| Estonia | Tallinn |
| Denmark | Copenhagen |
| Switzerland | Berne |
| Netherlands | Amsterdam |
| Moldova | Chișinău |
| Belgium | Brussels |
| Albania | Tirana |
| Macedonia | Skopje |
| Turkey | Istanbul |
| Slovenia | Ljubljana |
| Montenegro | Podgorica |
| Kosovo | Pristina |
| Cyprus | Nicosia |
| Azerbaijan | Baku |
| Luxembourg | Luxembourg |
| Georgia | Tbilisi |
| Andorra | Andorra la Vella |
| Malta | Valletta |
| Liechtenstein | Vaduz |
| San Marino | San Marino |
| Monaco | Monaco |
| Vatican City | Vatican City |

*Countries of Europe*

## RUSSIA

Welcome to the country that has territory in two continents, with about 25 per cent in Europe and the rest in Asia. The Ural Mountains form the border between the two territories.

So, is Russia considered a European country or an Asian country? Well, it is usually considered the part of a larger geographical entity called **Eurasia,** which covers both Europe and Asia. It is the largest country in the world by area and has a population of over 143 million people. More than 75 per cent of this population lives in European Russia. Christianity is the dominant religion in Russia and its currency is the Russian ruble.

**Capital City:** Moscow is the capital city of Russia and also the largest by both area and population. Earlier, St. Petersburg was the Russian capital.

**Must-see in Russia:** Take a look at Lake Baikal—the largest freshwater lake in the world. It has more than 20 per cent of the world's fresh surface water (we will visit it in Chapter 11).

## GERMANY

You're now in Germany, the second most populous country in Europe with over 82 million people. Germany is one of the most powerful and industrialized nations in Europe. It has, however, had a troubled history. It was part of the losing side in both World War I and World War II. In 1941–1945, Germany, then driven by Adolf Hitler's Nazi Party, led the Holocaust—the murder of 6 million Jewish people.

Present-day Germany is the world leader in several industries including engineering and automobiles. A majority of Germans are Christian. Most people speak German. The official currency is the euro, just like in eighteen other European countries.

**Capital City:** Berlin has been the capital of Germany since 1871. Did you know that Berlin was once divided into East and West Berlin? From 1961–1989, people could not cross over without permission. The wall still stands in places, but Berlin is now unified.

**Must-see in Germany:** Daydream at the Neuschwanstein Castle in Füssen. Its many towers and gorgeous fairytale-like construction was the inspiration for Walt Disney's theme parks.

## FRANCE

Ah, welcome to the world's hottest spot for fashion, romance and elegance! France is a politically powerful country that has rebuilt itself wonderfully after its losses in World War II. Many rivers flow through France, the longest of which is the Loire

River that runs for over 1000 km. Over 67 million people live in France, most of whom are Christians and speak French. The official currency of France is the euro.

**Capital City:** The French capital is Paris, fondly called the 'ville lumière' or 'city of light'. It is also the largest city in France, followed by Marseille and Lyon.

**Must-see in France:** Everyone knows about the Eiffel Tower, but make sure you visit the Palace of Versailles, about 20 km from Paris. It used to be the royal residence of the French ruler, Louis XIV. Even the word 'grand' would not do justice to describe the palace and its sprawling gardens. The palace has 2,300 rooms!

### UNITED KINGDOM

The UK is a special country in Europe. It is made of four member countries: England, Scotland, Wales and Northern Ireland. The UK is one of the most powerful nations in the world and has a long history of colonization. The British Empire is known to be the most extensive empire in world history. In the late 19th and early 20th centuries, it had colonies on all continents! Over 66 million people live in the UK today. The dominant religion is Christianity. The national currency is the pound sterling.

**Capital City:** London is the capital and largest city of the UK. Other large cities are Birmingham and Manchester.

**Must-see in the UK:** Explore the Stonehenge in Wiltshire, England. You'll see many stones about 3.9 m high. The structure was built more than 5000 years ago in 2000–3000 BC. Scientists believe the structure was used as a burial ground.

## THE COUNTRIES IN SOUTH AMERICA

Let's visit the next continent, ignoring icy Antarctica with zero countries. South America is divided into twelve countries. The largest is Brazil and the smallest is Suriname. Only 0.6 million people live in Suriname, South America's least densely populated country. Only seven people live every 2.5 sq km!

### LIST OF COUNTRIES IN SOUTH AMERICA
*(from largest to smallest by area)*

| COUNTRY | CAPITAL |
| --- | --- |
| Brazil | Brasília |
| Argentina | Buenos Aires |
| Peru | Lima |
| Columbia | Bogotá |
| Bolivia | Two capitals: Sucre and La Paz |
| Venezuela | Caracas |
| Chile | Santiago |
| Paraguay | Asunción |
| Ecuador | Quito |
| Guyana | Georgetown |
| Uruguay | Montevideo |
| Suriname | Paramaribo |

*Countries of South America*

## BRAZIL

Have you heard the incredibly catchy song 'To Brazil' by the Vengaboys in 1998? The energy of the song represents modern-day Brazil—a rapidly growing country that is becoming an economic power in world affairs. Brazil used to be a Portuguese colony. Today, 207 million people live here, many of whom are Americans, Africans and Europeans. Most people speak Portuguese.

Brazil is struggling to preserve the Amazon rainforest that covers much of its area due to reasons including overpopulation. The main religion in Brazil is Christianity. The official currency is the Brazilian real.

**Capital City:** Brasília is the capital of Brazil, and its third largest city after São Paulo and Rio de Janeiro.

**Must-see in Brazil:** Plan your trip to Brazil around the time of the Rio de Janeiro Carnival in February–March. It is the biggest carnival in the world that sees 2 million people revelling on the streets every day! It marks the period of celebration before Lent—a time when many Christians abstain from alcohol and meat.

## ARGENTINA

Welcome to one of the most resource-rich countries in South America! Through the country runs the fertile plains of the Pampas, and abundant reserves of iron ore, lead, copper and uranium. However, Argentina has been suffering from economic problems and debts that limit it from achieving its potential. It used to be a Spanish colony but became independent in 1816.

More than 44 million people live here, and most of them are Christians. The primary language is Spanish. The official currency is the Argentine peso.

**Capital City:** Buenos Aires is the Argentine capital and its largest city. Other big cities are Cordoba and Mendoza.

**Must-see in Argentina:** Be awestruck by the Iguazú Falls, one of the seven new natural wonders of the world. There are 257 individual falls here spread over 2.7 km!

## CHILE

Hola! That's 'hello' in Spanish. You're now in one of South America's most progressive and stable countries. Chile was a Spanish colony, but became independent in 1810.

Geographically, Chile is unique. As you can see on the map, it looks like a ribbon. The climate is as crazy as a cat's mood, from the hot and dry Atacama Desert to the snowy mountains of the Andes. About 18 million people live here. The main religion is Christianity, and the official currency is the Chilean peso.

**Capital City:** Santiago is the capital city of Chile, and also the largest. Other major cities are Puente Alto and Antofagasta.

**Must-see in Chile:** Navigate the Strait of Magellan. It is a sea route between the Atlantic and the Pacific Ocean. The route is named after Ferdinand Magellan, a Portuguese explorer who wanted to find a route from Spain to the Spice Islands in Indonesia. Sadly, he was killed during the voyage.

## THE COUNTRIES IN NORTH AMERICA

Onwards to the third largest continent in the world! North America is divided into 23 countries and several territories/regions. The United States and Canada are the biggest countries in this continent, and take up almost 79 per cent of the area. The smallest country—Saint Kitts and Nevis—has an area of only 269.4 sq km.

As you can see in the map, Greenland is also located in North America. It is the world's largest island. But remember that even though Greenland is located in North America, it is actually a territory of Denmark in Europe.

### LIST OF COUNTRIES IN NORTH AMERICA
*(from largest to smallest by area)*

| COUNTRY | CAPITAL |
| --- | --- |
| Canada | Ottawa |
| United States of America | Washington, D.C. |
| Mexico | Mexico City |
| Nicaragua | Managua |

| Honduras | Tegucigalpa |
| --- | --- |
| Cuba | Havana |
| Guatemala | Guatemala City |
| Panama | Panama City |
| Costa Rica | San Jose |
| Dominican Republic | Santo Domingo |
| Haiti | Port-au-Prince |
| Belize | Belmopan |
| El Salvador | San Salvador |
| Bahamas | Nassau |
| Jamaica | Kingston |
| Trinidad and Tobago | Port of Spain |
| Dominica | Roseau |
| Saint Lucia | Castries |
| Antigua and Barbuda | Saint John's |
| Barbados | Bridgetown |
| Saint Vincent | Kingstown |
| Grenada | Saint George's |
| Saint Kitts and Nevis | Basseterre |

*Countries of North America*

## CANADA

Greetings from the largest North American country! Canada has the highest number of lakes in the world—2 million! It is also famous for its polite people and a developed economy that welcomes immigrants. Did you know that the Hudson Bay Area in Canada has less gravity than the rest of the Earth?

About 37 million people live in Canada. The dominant religion is Christianity, while the primary languages are English and French. The official currency is the Canadian dollar.

**Capital City:** The capital of Canada is Ottawa, and not Toronto! Toronto is, however, the largest city followed by Montreal and Vancouver. Queen Victoria made the city of Ottawa the capital in 1857, since it is centrally located between Montreal and Toronto.

**Must-see in Canada:** Ever wanted to meet a polar bear? Visit Churchill in Canada; it's called the 'Polar Bear Capital of the World'. But, be warned—polar bears are hardly as cute and gentle as they look! If provoked, they can become extremely violent.

## UNITED STATES OF AMERICA

Considered to be one of the world's most powerful countries, the US is also the third largest after Russia and Canada. It is the world's largest economy. The United States was part of the British Empire until 1776, when it became independent. Modern-day America is a trendsetter in entertainment, famous for Hollywood or the US film industry.

About 327 million people live in the US. The dominant religion is Christianity. Though many people speak English, the US has no official language. Spanish, Chinese and French are also widely spoken languages there. The official currency is the United States dollar.

**Capital City:** Washington, D.C. is the capital of the US. 'D.C.' stands for 'District of Columbia'. It is a unique capital because it was specially established by the country's constitution. The largest city in the US is New York.

Why are there thirteen stripes on the US flag?

The thirteen stripes stand for the first thirteen British colonies that declared independence from the British Empire, and became US states.

**Must-see in the US:** Explore the icy wilderness of Alaska. The US bought Alaska from Russia back in 1867 for a price of $7.2 million. The sparsely populated state is full of glaciers, icy rivers, forests and bears!

## MEXICO

The country of Mexico is a study in extremes! It has affluence, but also dire poverty, with many crossing the border to the US for jobs. Mexico suffers from the problem of 'drug cartels' (illegal groups that transport addictive drugs). Innocent people die in acts of gang violence. Drug addiction can be very dangerous; it can have a serious impact on someone's health and mental well-being.

More than 123 million people live in Mexico. Christianity is the dominant religion, and Spanish is the most spoken language. In Mexico, the official currency is the Mexican peso.

**Capital City:** Mexico City is the capital of Mexico and also its largest city. Other big cities are Guadalajara and Monterrey.

**Must-see in Mexico:** The Pyramids. What?! Aren't the Pyramids in Egypt, Africa? Well, the Great Pyramid of Cholula in Mexico is the world's largest pyramid with a volume of 4.45 million cbm. The Great Pyramid of Egypt has a volume of only 2.5 million cbm.

## THE COUNTRIES IN AFRICA

Your trip has now brought you to the continent with the maximum number of countries in the world. There are as many as fifty-four! While Algeria is the largest country in Africa, the small island nation of Seychelles is the smallest. Seychelles is an archipelago, a group of 115 islands in the Indian Ocean. Thousands of tourists visit each year to see the Aldabra giant tortoise, one of the largest tortoises in the world.

### LIST OF COUNTRIES IN AFRICA
*(from largest to smallest by area)*

| COUNTRY | CAPITAL |
| --- | --- |
| Algeria | Algiers |
| Democratic Republic of the Congo | Kinshasa |
| Sudan | Juba |
| Libya | Tripoli |

| Chad | N'Djamena |
|------|-----------|
| Niger | Niamey |
| Angola | Luanda |
| Mali | Bamako |
| South Africa | Three capitals: Pretoria, Cape Town and Bloemfontein |
| Ethiopia | Addis Ababa |
| Mauritania | Nouakchott |
| Egypt | Cairo |
| Tanzania | Dodoma |
| Nigeria | Abuja |
| Namibia | Windhoek |
| Mozambique | Maputo |
| Zambia | Lusaka |
| South Sudan | Juba |
| Somalia | Mogadishu |
| Central African Republic | Bangui |
| Madagascar | Antananarivo |
| Botswana | Gaborone |
| Kenya | Nairobi |
| Cameroon | Yaounde |
| Morocco | Rabat |
| Zimbabwe | Harare |
| Republic of the Congo | Brazzaville |
| Ivory Coast | Yamoussoukro |
| Burkina Faso | Ouagadougou |
| Gabon | Libreville |

| | |
|---|---|
| Guinea | Conakry |
| Ghana | Accra |
| Uganda | Kampala |
| Senegal | Dakar |
| Tunisia | Tunis |
| Malawi | Lilongwe |
| Eritrea | Asmara |
| Benin | Porto Novo |
| Liberia | Monrovia |
| Sierra Leone | Freetown |
| Togo | Lomé |
| Guinea-Bissau | Bissau |
| Lesotho | Maseru |
| Equatorial Guinea | Two capitals: Malabo and Oyala |
| Burundi | Bujumbura |
| Rwanda | Kigali |
| Djibouti | Djibouti |
| Eswatini | Two capitals: Mbabane and Lobamba |
| Gambia | Banjul |
| Cape Verde | Praia |
| Comoros | Moroni |
| Mauritius | Port Louis |
| São Tomé and Príncipe | São Tomé |
| Seychelles | Victoria |

*Countries of Africa*

## NIGERIA

Welcome to Nigeria, one of the largest oil producers in the world. As of 2018, Nigeria is not only the wealthiest but also the most populous country in Africa. Even so, the country faces severe economic, political and social challenges. In recent years, many of these challenges have been due to a militant organization called Boko Haram. This organization started with the goal to 'purify' the religion of Islam in Nigeria, but has since engaged in terrorism and killed thousands of people.

Over 186 million people live in Nigeria. Most of them practise two main religions: Islam and Christianity. People speak English as well as the local languages of Hausa, Yoruba and Igbo. The Nigerian naira is the official currency.

**Capital City:** The capital city is Abuja and the largest city is Lagos.

**Must-see in Nigeria:** Walk inside the Osun-Osogbo Sacred Grove situated along the Oşun river. Nigerians believe that Oşun, the Goddess of Fertility, resides here. The forest also contains 400 species of medicinal plants.

## SOUTH AFRICA

If you're a cricket fan, you must have seen the South African team do great things on the field. The country of South Africa is one of the most developed economies of the continent. It is also famous for abolishing apartheid, the discrimination based on race that existed in the country till 1994.

South Africa is a geographically varied country. It has deserts, grasslands, wetlands, forests, as well as mountains. The Table Mountain in Cape Town is one of the oldest mountains in the world. It is full of running dassies—little animals that look like rabbits.

About 57 million people live in South Africa and practise Christianity, the dominant religion there. People speak many languages including English, Zulu, Swati and Venda. Aren't the names fascinating? The official currency of this country is the South African rand.

**Capital City:** South Africa is unique even in the concept of capital cities—it is the only country that has three! Pretoria is the administrative capital, Cape Town the legislative capital, and Bloemfontein the judicial capital.

**Must-see in South Africa:** After you're done with the great wildlife safari, explore the Cape of Good Hope near the Table Mountain. You can watch majestic birds like the cormorants and ostriches. Did you know that cormorants are such excellent swimmers that they can dive 30 m into the water to catch fish? That's some serious fish-love!

## EGYPT

Most people have dreamed about exploring the ancient country of Egypt, with its spectacular pyramids and gleaming deserts. There are many settlements in the delta of the Nile. Lately, Egypt has been struggling with political turmoil which has taken a toll on its economy and natural resources.

Out of the 100 million people who live here, most practise Islam and speak Arabic. The Egyptian pound is the official currency.

**Capital City:** Cairo is the Egyptian capital and the biggest city. Alexandria is another large city in Egypt. Interestingly, the status of the capital of Cairo is under threat. As of 2018, Mr Abdel Fattah el-Sisi, the current president of Egypt, was building a new capital city for Egypt, whose name is yet to be decided.

**Must-see in Egypt:** Everyone knows about the Pyramids of Giza. But when in Egypt, you shouldn't miss the White Desert in Farafra. The sand is totally white here, and you can see calcium rock formations that look exactly like mushrooms and ice creams. When the moonlight shines at night, everything looks even more white—almost like the surface of the moon!

## THE COUNTRIES IN ASIA

Ah, you've finally arrived hale and hearty to the last leg of your inter-country tour across the Earth. Welcome once again to Asia, the largest continent in the world. Close on the heels of Africa, the continent of Asia has an enormous number of countries—fifty-one! Russia is its biggest country while the Maldives, a stunning island country with an area of only 300 sq km, is its smallest.

You will notice that some countries like Georgia appear in the list of countries of both Europe and Asia. This is because these countries have territories in both the continents. They are sometimes referred to as part of a larger geographical entity called Eurasia (Europe + Asia).

Did you see how Singapore is the capital of Singapore? It is very much like the Vatican City in Europe—the country that is its own capital. These countries are called '**city-states**'. They are cities that form an independent country. Monaco in Europe is another example of a city-state.

### LIST OF COUNTRIES IN ASIA
*(from largest to smallest by area)*

| CAPITAL | COUNTRY |
|---------|---------|
| Russia | Moscow |
| China | Beijing |
| India | New Delhi |
| Kazakhstan | Astana |
| Saudi Arabia | Riyadh |
| Iran | Tehran |

| | |
|---|---|
| Mongolia | Ulaanbaatar |
| Indonesia | Jakarta |
| Pakistan | Islamabad |
| Turkey | Ankara |
| Myanmar | Naypyidaw |
| Afghanistan | Kabul |
| Yemen | Sana'a |
| Thailand | Bangkok |
| Turkmenistan | Ashgabat |
| Uzbekistan | Tashkent |
| Iraq | Baghdad |
| Japan | Tokyo |
| Vietnam | Hanoi |
| Malaysia | Kuala Lumpur |
| Oman | Muscat |
| Philippines | Manila |
| Laos | Vientiane |
| Kyrgyzstan | Bishkek |
| Syria | Damascus |
| Cambodia | Phnom Penh |
| Bangladesh | Dhaka |
| Nepal | Kathmandu |
| Tajikistan | Dushanbe |
| North Korea | Pyongyang |
| South Korea | Seoul |
| Jordan | Amman |
| Azerbaijan | Baku |
| United Arab Emirates | Abu Dhabi |
| Georgia | Tbilisi |

| Sri Lanka | Two capitals: Colombo and Sri Jayawardenepura Kotte |
| --- | --- |
| Egypt | Cairo |
| Bhutan | Thimphu |
| Taiwan | Taipei |
| Armenia | Yerevan |
| Israel | Jerusalem |
| Kuwait | Kuwait City |
| Timor-Leste | Dili |
| Qatar | Doha |
| Lebanon | Beirut |
| Cyprus | Nicosia |
| Palestine | Two capitals: Ramallah and East Jerusalem |
| Brunei | Bandar Seri Begawan |
| Bahrain | Manama |
| Singapore | Singapore |
| Maldives | Malé |

*Countries of Asia*

## JAPAN

Kon'nichiwa! That's 'hello' in Japanese! You're now in one of the most developed and technologically advanced countries in the world. Japan has grown tremendously after its terrible losses in World War II. But did you know that Japan is actually an archipelago? An archipelago is a group of islands. The country of Japan is a group of about 6,852 islands of which only 430 are inhabited! Spring in Japan is like a modern fairytale, when the country is full of pink cherry blossoms. These flowers bloom for only about a week and the period is called 'Sakura Snow'.

About 127 million people live in Japan. Shinto and Buddhism are the main religions, while the official currency is the yen. Most people speak Japanese, which is also considered one of the most difficult languages to learn. It is, however, a beautiful language with words that cannot be translated into English.

### Do you know what 'boketto' means?

In Japanese, boketto means gazing into the distance without thinking. Now that's something most of us have been guilty of doing in the classroom!

**Capital City:** Tokyo is the capital and largest city of Japan. Yokohama and Osaka are other large cities.

**Must-see in Japan:** How would you like to visit an active volcano that could burst anytime? Mount Fuji in Japan is an active volcano and one of the most popular tourist sites. It last erupted in 1707, but you never know!

## INDIA

Namastey! You're now in the largest democracy in the world. A **democracy** is a system of government in which the people choose their political leaders, and the elected representatives form the governing body. India is a geographically diverse country, from the Sunderbans to the Thar desert, the fertile Indo-Gangetic Plain to the Himalayan range.

India attained independence from British rule in 1947 and has since grown considerably. It continues to face territorial disputes with the neighbouring country of Pakistan and also grapples with economic problems.

As many as 1.32 billion people live in India, second only to China that has the largest population in the world (1.41 billion). Hinduism, Islam, Christianity and Sikhism are some of the main religions. The Indian Constitution recognizes twenty-two languages! People speak Hindi, Bengali, Tamil, Gujarati, Marathi and many more beautiful languages. The official currency is the Indian rupee.

**Capital City:** New Delhi is the capital city of India. Other main cities include Mumbai, Bengaluru and Kolkata.

**Must-see in India:** Trek to the Valley of Flowers in Chamoli in the state of Uttarakhand. The valley is a colourful riot of flowers, little waterfalls, and great soft beds of green grass. It is situated at a height of 3,658 m above sea level.

# CHINA

The last country you'll travel to on this inter-country tour is also the most widely populated country on Earth. China has grown to become one of the top exporters in the world. It exports machinery, textiles, minerals, toys and many other products. The Yangtze river, which is the world's third largest river after the Nile and the Amazon, flows through this country.

Most people in this country of 1.4 billion people speak Mandarin. Buddhism is the primary religion. The official currency is the renminbi, also known as the Chinese yuan.

**Capital City:** Beijing is the capital of China, although, Shanghai is its largest city.

What is the difference between communism and socialism?

In a communist society, the community or the people own the means of production. But in a socialist society, the government owns the means of production.

**Must-see in China:** Check out the Forbidden City in Beijing. It is a palace spread over 720,000 sq m and has 8728 rooms. It used to be the emperor's palace in China. At one time, the palace guards were particular about who was allowed to enter. Some people say that even the emperor's mother was made to wait at the gates! But don't worry; it isn't forbidden anymore.

## EXERCISE 2: HIGHLIGHTS FROM YOUR INTER-COUNTRY TRIP

Bet your base station looks appealing after that long but exciting trip! Study the maps below and show off your traveller's experience by identifying the countries that are sketched here.

1.

The capital city of this country was once divided into 'East' and 'West' by a wall. Name the country and the continent._____

2.

You can't see the Amazon rainforest on the map, but we're sure you know which country it is in. Write it here:_____

3.

The flag of this country has an eagle, a serpent and a cactus! Write down the name of the country and the continent._____

4.

This country witnesses a beautiful phenomenon called 'Sakura Snow'. Which country is it?_____

5.

The capital city of the country shown on the map is Suva. Can you name the country?_____

6.

This country is famous for a sea route called the Strait of Magellan. Which country is it?_____

7.

This country has not one or two, but three capitals! Name it._____

8.

On the flag of this country are four red stars. Do you know which country it is?_____

9.

This highly populated country has a 'Forbidden City'. Write down the name of the country and the continent here._____

10.

The people of this country speak interesting languages such as Hausa, Yoruba and Igbo. Which country is it?_____

11.

The official flag of this country is called the Union Jack. Do you know its name?_____

12.

Doesn't this country look huge? It is the third largest country on Earth. Name it._____

# OCEANS OF THE WORLD

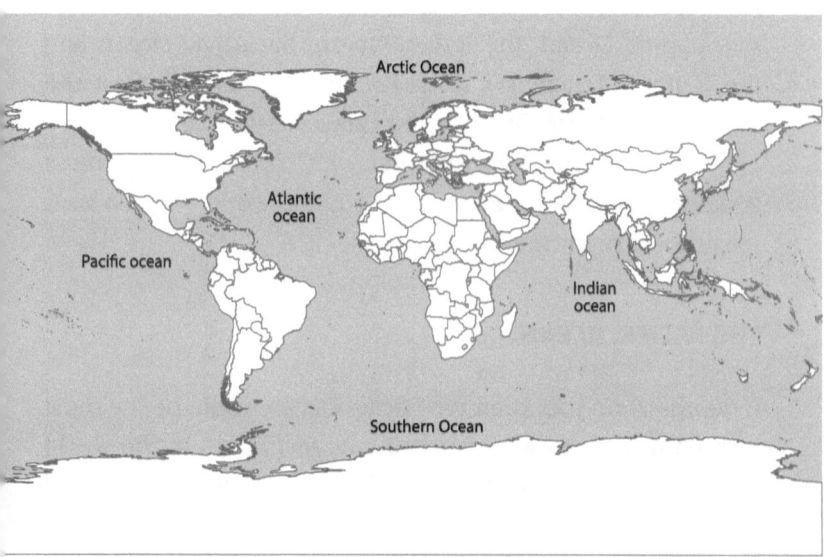

*The world's oceans*

We live on the Blue Planet where 71 per cent of the surface is covered by water. The massive water bodies flowing across the Earth's surface make life possible on this planet. These water bodies contain saline or salty water and are called **oceans**. Earth is the only known planet to have water in the liquid form on its surface. Some scientists believe that liquid water exists on Mars, but we know nothing yet for sure.

Can you imagine life without water to drink? Human

beings can live without food for weeks. But without water, you won't live for more than three-four days. Without water, neither plants nor animals can survive. Millions of people whose livelihood depends on fishing and shipping would go without an income. The great oceans are extremely important!

Our world is divided into **five** oceans: the Pacific Ocean, the Atlantic Ocean, the Indian Ocean, the Arctic Ocean and the Southern Ocean. While the Pacific Ocean is the largest and deepest, the Arctic Ocean is the smallest and shallowest.

Have you grabbed your oars yet? We are going on a thrilling ride across the five oceans of the world, so keep your seasickness medicine close!

### THE PACIFIC OCEAN

If depths scare you, then the Pacific Ocean would be the most horrifying body of water! It is the largest ocean in the world with an area of 165,200,000 sq km. Compare this with the area of Delhi in India, which is only 1,484 sq km. The Pacific Ocean is more than 1,00,000 times bigger! This ocean flows to the west of North and South America and the east of Asia and Australia.

With an average depth of more than 3,973 m, the Pacific Ocean is also the deepest ocean in the world. Here, you will find the deepest spot on Earth—the Mariana Trench, with a depth of 10,970 m! In 2012, James Cameron, the director of the Hollywood blockbuster movie *Titanic*, went down into the Mariana Trench in a big submarine called the Deepsea Challenger. He was the first to perform this solo voyage. Wonder if he had his heart in his mouth the whole time!

## What's the Temperature Like?

If you are planning on taking a dip in the ocean, be careful of the temperature fluctuations. The water is warm near the tropics (28–32°C), but it can get below freezing near the poles. Even deep below, the temperature of the water is usually only a few degrees, unless you are near a volcanic vent. What?! Volcanoes under the water? Yes, there is an entire string of underwater volcanoes in the Pacific Ocean. It is called the Ring of Fire.

## What Are the Life Forms Here?

Watch out for the hammerhead shark! It is very common in the Pacific waters; you can recognize it by its unique hammer-shaped head. Some species of the hammerhead shark like the great hammerhead are dangerous to human beings. Killer whales (or orcas) and humpback whales also live in the ocean. They are likely to leave you alone, but it is a bad idea to disturb them!

Other inhabitants include sea otters, turtles, sea lions, octopuses, squids and slugs. Many of them eat algae, seaweeds and sea lettuce. Sounds gross? Well, many humans eat seaweeds too. Seaweeds have nutrients like magnesium and iron.

## ATLANTIC OCEAN

Onwards to the second largest ocean in the world! The Atlantic Ocean is not far behind the Pacific Ocean in terms of area, as it spreads across 106,400,000 sq km. It is also terrifyingly deep, with an average depth of 3,660 m. To its west are North and

South America and to its east are Europe and Africa. Many seas such as the Mediterranean Sea, the Caribbean Sea and the Baltic Sea are part of the Atlantic Ocean.

## Can You Guess the Difference Between an Ocean and a Sea?

Seas are much smaller than oceans. Seas are usually located at the point where an ocean meets the land.

Hundreds of ships and sailors have disappeared in a mysterious area of the Atlantic Ocean, never to be found again. On your voyage through these waters, you might want to steer clear of the **Bermuda Triangle,** also known as the Devil's Triangle. It is roughly bordered by Miami, Bermuda and Puerto Rico. But don't worry; it is more likely that the hurricanes are causing the accidents and not the devil.

Underneath the Atlantic Ocean is a world of wonder. You will find a mountain range called the Mid-Atlantic Ridge. At 16,000 km, it is the longest mountain range in the world! The Andes, or the longest above-land mountain range on Earth, is only about 7,000 km long. This ocean is also full of **icebergs** from February to August. These masses of ice get detached from glaciers and float loosely. If they appear to be not-so-large above the water, don't be fooled! Almost 90 per cent of their body is underneath! It was an iceberg that sank the Titanic, one of the biggest ships of our times, back in 1912. The ship now rests deep under the Atlantic Ocean.

## What's the Temperature Like?

Most of the Atlantic Ocean is cold except the areas near the equator. The average temperatures range between -2°C and 30°C. The ocean is getting colder due to a phenomenon called the Atlantic Multidecadal Oscillation (AMO). The AMO is influenced by trends in average rainfall and temperature, and affects the temperature of this ocean every few decades.

## What Are the Life Forms Here?

Get ready to greet some of your friends from the Pacific Ocean again! The Atlantic Ocean is home to humpback whales, killer whales, sea turtles, sea horses and seals. It is also home to some distinctive species of animals that you won't find anywhere else.

Steer miles and miles away from the great white shark, a deadly shark that has been involved in a huge number of human attacks. They have 300 teeth, and we bet you wouldn't like to see them up close. You might feel safer with the lemon shark that has a yellowish-green body colour and is relatively less aggressive.

The sperm whale, which is the largest living toothed animal in the world, lives in the Atlantic Ocean. Sadly, its relationship with humans has not been very amicable. Due to its vast reserves of body oil, people hunted this whale so much that the species was endangered!

The plant life in the Atlantic Ocean is similar to that of the Pacific Ocean. Other than grass, algae and phytoplankton, you will also find a plant called kelp. It is a type of large brown seaweed that can grow up to a height of 61 m.

### INDIAN OCEAN

If someone told you that the spices you like eating in your food actually came from the Indian Ocean, you might laugh out loud. From nutmeg and cloves to black pepper, the Indian

Ocean has always been a supplier of rich spices to the world! A group of islands in this ocean, aptly called 'Spice Islands,' was once coveted by explorers around the world. Today, they are called the Maluku Islands in Indonesia and form a part of the 73,556,000 sq km of the Indian Ocean.

The third largest ocean on Earth, the Indian Ocean has an average depth of 3,962 m. To its north lies Asia and to its west lies Africa. Indonesia and Australia lie to its east. It extends southwards to the continent of Antarctica.

Geologists believe that deep inside the Indian Ocean, there is a lost continent! It is believed to exist under the island nation of Mauritius, which is why they have named it 'Mauritia.'

Unfortunately, the Indian Ocean is severely polluted, which means a death sentence for the animals and plants living in the water. Scientists believe that about 1 trillion pieces of rubbish are floating around in this ocean. One trillion equals a million millions!

## What's the Temperature Like?

The Indian Ocean is the warmest among all oceans. The average temperature is in the range of 22°C–27°C in the upper layers. While this sounds pleasant for a dip, it is not liked by many species of phytoplankton who find it difficult to grow in warm waters.

## What Are the Life Forms Here?

Deep inside the Indian Ocean, you might come face-to-face with a colourful little anemone-fish called the Chagos. It is light to dark brown in colour. Do you know why they are called anemone-fish? It is because they live within sea anemones, never going more than a few metres away from their host.

Swimming placidly through the waters is the blue whale, the largest mammal on Earth. They weight 1,40,000 kg and an elephant that you may find really heavy weighs only 3,000–6,000 kg! When compared to the Atlantic and the Pacific, the variety of flora and fauna in this ocean is limited.

## SOUTHERN OCEAN

Brrr! You're now in the coldest ocean of the world! And no wonder, for it flows in and around Antarctica, the coldest continent. The Southern Ocean is the fourth largest ocean of the world, with an area of 20,327,000 sq km. It has an average depth of more than 3,962 m.

The Southern Ocean is also the newest ocean. It was not even considered a separate ocean until the year 2000. Scientists used to call these waters the 'adjoining waters of the Pacific, Atlantic and Indian oceans'. But then, it was decided that the ocean would get its own identity, and so, it was named the Southern Ocean or the Antarctic Ocean.

On the surface of the Southern Ocean, you'll find many icebergs. Did you know that icebergs are a great source of fresh water? While you cannot drink sea water because it is salty, icebergs are formed of snow, which is fresh water.

### What's the Temperature Like?

No surprises here, and no, your thickest swimsuits aren't likely to be enough! The Southern Ocean is supremely cold, since it is close to the South Pole. The average temperature of these waters ranges from -2°C to 10°C.

## What Are the Life Forms Here?

You would think no animals could survive in such extreme temperatures. But surprisingly, many animals manage just fine! Perhaps the grandest is the emperor penguin that you won't find anywhere else in the world. It cannot fly, but it is a superb swimmer and diver. Alongside the penguin, you can also find aquatic birds like the albatross and gulls.

The blue whale that you met in the Indian Ocean is present in abundant numbers here. It loves these waters because inside the Southern Ocean is its favourite food—the Antarctic krill. The krill is a crustacean, which means it is a member of the same family as crabs, lobsters and shrimps.

### ARCTIC OCEAN

You're now at the final stage of your oceanic ride. In front of you is the smallest and shallowest ocean of the world—the Arctic Ocean. It has an area of 13,986,000 sq km and a mean depth of about 1,067 m. Around the Arctic Ocean are the continents of Europe, North America and Asia.

The Arctic Ocean is also freezing. Most of the ocean is covered by ice throughout the year, which makes it difficult to pass through these waters. When ships need to go through, an icebreaker ship has to accompany them!

## What's the Temperature Like?

The Arctic Ocean has an average temperature of -2°C. For most of the year, the sea is full of ice and icebergs. The islands in this ocean are full of permafrost. Permafrost is frozen sand. In recent times, the ice has been melting due to rising temperatures on Earth. This is called **global warming**, and it is very dangerous. Imagine what would happen if all the ice were to melt and the level of the oceans were to rise. There would be floods all over!

## What Are the Life Forms Here?

Say hello to polar bears! These furry creatures live exclusively in the Arctic region and walk over the ice to hunt down their favourite food—seals. The rise in global warming poses a serious threat to polar bears. How will they survive if the ice melts?

The Arctic Ocean is also home to some of the most exciting creatures you will find on Earth. Skulking around somewhere is the Arctic fox with snow white fur. This animal is so resilient that it can survive in temperatures as extreme as 50°C!

Swimming along steadily in the waters of the Arctic Ocean is the beluga or the white whale. These whales love talking with the help of different sounds. So impressive are their vocalizations that they are fondly called 'sea canaries' after the famous singing bird from the Macaronesian Islands in the Atlantic Ocean.

Another whale found in these waters is the bowhead whale, also known as the Greenland right whale. It has a comb-like mouth that can filter the water to catch planktons. How very useful!

The skies above the Arctic Ocean mostly remain dark. During the winters, it gets even darker. But the Arctic terns and the snow geese are birds that don't mind this gloomy weather. They happily fly about in this region.

## EXERCISE 3: HIGHLIGHTS FROM YOUR OCEANIC TRIP

Welcome back to dry land after hours of swimming about and shipping through the great oceans! Identify the oceans in the map below (1–5). Use capital letters to write the names of the largest and smallest oceans, and specify which is which with the help of arrows.

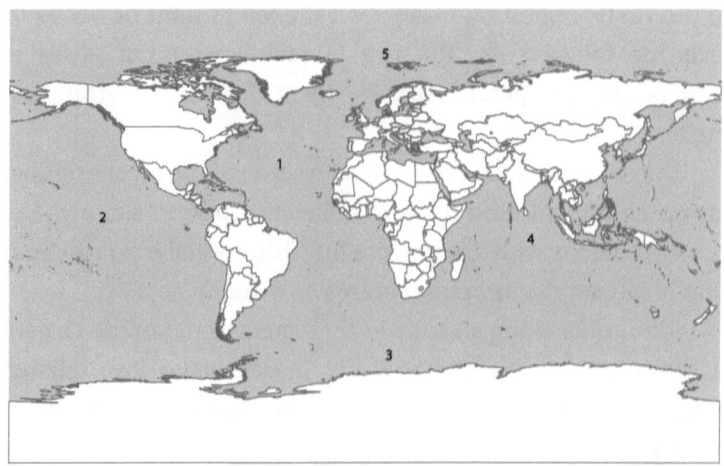

1. _____
2. _____
3. _____
4. _____
5. _____

# MOUNTAIN RANGES OF THE WORLD

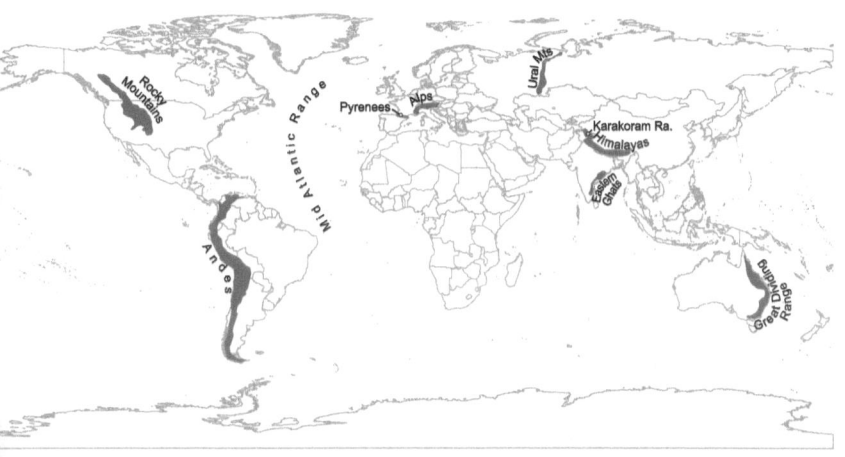

*Mountain ranges*

Have you ever flown in an aeroplane? Doesn't the world appear tiny from up there, with the cars looking like toys and the houses like matchboxes? You can see a similar sight if you trek up to some of the high and mighty mountains. When a group or chain of mountains exists close together, it is called a **mountain range.**

There are many mountain ranges in the world—too many to count! Some geologists consider only those mountains that have a height of at least 304 m. Otherwise, even the tiny hills in your backyard that you climb up in minutes would count as mountains.

Mountains get formed when the tectonic plates (slabs of solid rock) of the Earth smash against each other. These plates keep moving due to geological activities under the Earth's surface—a process called plate tectonics. Sometimes, mountains form when volcanoes erupt. The magma or molten lava gets pushed out from deep under the Earth. As the magma cools, it turns into hard rock.

Mountains and mountain ranges can be found all over the Earth's surface and even deep inside the oceans. Let's trek up to some of the major mountain ranges of our planet and explore the world from high up in the clouds.

## THE ANDES: THE LONGEST MOUNTAIN RANGE ON LAND

Imagine a chain of mountains that runs for 7,000 km. That's the Andes! It is the world's largest mountain range and is found in South America. If you go to South America, you can visit the Andes from all the seven countries it cuts through: Chile, Peru, Argentina, Ecuador, Venezuela, Columbia and Bolivia.

Beware of the volcanoes though, for the Andes is full of them, and some of them are even active! The Ojos del Salado on the Argentina-Chile border is the highest active volcano in the world, at a height of 6,893 m.

### Hall of Fame: Major Peaks

The highest mountain in the Andes is Mount Aconcagua in Argentina. It has a height of 6,961 m, only a little higher than the Ojos del Salado. The third highest peak in the Andes is the Monte Pissis, also in Argentina. It has a height of 6,793 m.

## Life in the Mountains

The Andes is full of biodiversity—you will find glaciers as well as rainforests; deserts as well as lakes. The climate ranges from severely cold in the Antarctic regions to warm as you approach the equator. Look out for the large predatory animals that live in the Andes forests. It is quite common to find jaguars and bears.

Life in the Andes mountains isn't easy. Temperatures can be extreme, and you need special fur coats to survive! That is why chinchillas love this place. They are rodents that look a lot like mice, except for their thick fur coat. Llamas and alpacas also live in the Andes. They look very much like winter camels.

The most notable plant of the Andes is the Cinchona pubescens. It is used to produce quinine. Quinine is the medicine for malaria, a serious mosquito-borne illness.

## THE HIMALAYAS: THE TALLEST MOUNTAIN RANGE

Over 200 people have died trying to climb Mount Everest, which is the tallest mountain in the world, at a height of 8,848 m. It isn't just the height that killed them, but also the shallow oxygen levels and the icy cold weather. And yet, many mountaineers attempt to climb the Mount Everest and other tall peaks of the Himalayan mountain range every year.

The Himalayas cover around 2,400 km. They stretch across six countries in Asia: India, Pakistan, Afghanistan, China, Bhutan and Nepal. Their location is particularly favourable for India. In the winter, the mountains stop the cold air from bringing severe winter to India.

## Hall of Fame: Major Peaks

It isn't just Mount Everest that gets all the attention in the Himalayas. Almost thirty mountains are more than 7,000 m high! The second tallest mountain in the Himalayas is the Kangchenjunga, with a height of 8,586 m. Do you know what its name means? It means 'five treasures of high snow'. The Kangchenjunga mountain has five peaks. The Himalayas also include Mount Kailash in Tibet, China. It is said to be the home of the Hindu deity Shiva.

## Life in the Mountains

The Himalayan range varies sharply in height. At various levels, you will find different climates—from warm to below freezing. According to the climate, there are various kinds of trees. While rhododendrons grow on the slopes of mountains, you can find oaks, palms, figs and chestnuts at different altitudes.

One of the fascinating creatures of the Himalayas is the snow leopard, with its thick grey fur. They are wonderful predators and think nothing of walking barefoot on the snow!

The Himalayas are also home to many innocent animals that prefer to live in the calm and quiet, like the Himalayan tahr, a kind of wild goat, and the Himalayan blue sheep that surprisingly has a grey-brown coat. Biologists say that this animal is more closely related to the goat than sheep.

## THE KARAKORAM: THE SECOND TALLEST MOUNTAIN RANGE

Wait, isn't the Karakoram range a part of the Himalayas? No, but it is very close to the Himalayas. If you go to a little town called Gilgit in Pakistan, you can see the point where three major mountain ranges of the world meet: the Himalayas, the Karakoram and the Hindu Kush. This mountain range spans 500 km and passes through five countries: Pakistan, India, China, Afghanistan and Tajikistan.

The Karakoram range is important because of a very special peak: the K2. It is the second tallest mountain in the world after Mount Everest, and has a height of 8,611 m.

## Is K2 Taller Than Mount Everest?

Some people believe that K2 is taller than Mount Everest during winter. This is because it gets so much snow that its height increases. While this isn't true, K2 can be harder to climb because of its even worse weather and sudden storms.

You would think that at heights like these, making roads and building houses are impossible. But high up in the mountains is the China-Pakistan Friendship Highway, extending for 1,300 km. It is the highest paved road in the world.

## Hall of Fame: Major Peaks

After the K2, the second highest mountain in the Karakoram range is the Gasherbrum I. It has a height of 8,080 m. Doesn't it have a fascinating name? It means 'shining wall'. The Gasherbrum I is also called K5. The third highest peak in the Karakoram range is the Broad Peak with an elevation of 8,051 m.

## Life in the Mountains

Many areas up in the Karakoram range are severely cold and glaciated. Depending on the elevation, you can experience warm summers, cool autumns and cold winters. Alongside streams, you can find trees of willow, poplar and oleander.

The animals prowling about in the Karakoram range belong to similar families as in the Himalayas. There are bears, snow leopards, sheep and goats. The Siberian ibex can often be spotted here. Thanks to its long horns and beard, you cannot miss it! The male ibexes have longer beards than the females.

## THE ALPS: THE HIGHEST MOUNTAIN RANGE IN EUROPE

Have you seen the blockbuster English movie *The Sound of Music*? It is about a woman named Maria who is sent to become the governess of seven children. If you have seen it, you must have marvelled at the beautiful mountains in the movie. They were part of the Alps mountain range, the permanently snow-covered range that is also the tallest in Europe. This mountain range covers about 1,200 km and spans eight countries: Switzerland, Austria, Germany, France, Italy, Liechtenstein, Monaco and Slovenia.

Here and there in this range, you can see spectacular, crystal-clear lakes. Lake Geneva, a lake between France and Switzerland, that has an area of 580 sq km, is the largest.

### Hall of Fame: Major Peaks

You must have heard about the tallest mountain in this range. It is called Mont Blanc—yes, the German luxury pens are named after this mountain. It has a height of 4,809 m. The second tallest is Mount Rosa, with a height of 4,634 m. It is the tallest mountain in Switzerland.

## Life in the Mountains

The Alps are severely cold, but as you descend, trees and forests begin to grow. You can easily find beautiful oak and chestnut trees along with pine and spruce. The people who live in the Alps produce some of the best cheese in the world!

You would have already met many of the animals that live in the Alpine regions. The ibexes and wild goats lounge about in the mountains, passing their days in quiet contentment. But look out for the European lynx. It is a member of the cat family and loves to hunt down deer and goats.

Hiding in the Alps are also some little creatures that disappear in the blink of an eye. Skulking about are otters, badgers, squirrels, hares and shrews. Have you seen small shrews walk with their mother? They all walk in a line, holding the tail of the one in front, in their mouth. It is quite a cute little procession if you're lucky enough to witness one!

## THE ROCKIES: THE LONGEST MOUNTAIN RANGE IN NORTH AMERICA

Let's vroom to North America and look at the mountain ranges of this great continent. Spanning 4,800 km is the Rockies, the longest mountain range in North America, and the second longest in the entire world after the Andes. These mountains stretch across three countries: Canada, the US and Mexico.

On your trip, make sure to visit the Columbia Icefield, a huge field of ice that supplies ice to several big glaciers in Canada. One of the most popular glaciers among tourists is the Athabasca Glacier, which is also shrinking by the minute due to global warming.

Many areas of these mountains are now protected and have been made into national parks like the Yellowstone National Park in the Rockies of the US. It has the world's most famous geyser with a lovely name—Old Faithful Geyser. Every forty-four to 125 minutes, it is sure to erupt faithfully!

## Hall of Fame: Major Peaks

The highest peak of the Rockies is Mount Elbert, at a height of 4,401 m. The second and third highest peaks are Mount Massive and Mount Harvard respectively. Interestingly, all the top three peaks are located in the state of Colorado, in the US.

## Life in the Mountains

Like the Andes, the Rockies is also biodiverse and has several climatic zones. You can find wetlands, alpine regions as well as coniferous forests here. This is why many flowering plants such as wild roses and junipers bloom here.

The Rockies are home to mountain animals including sheep, bears, lynxes and mountain goats. You can also see interesting species of deer called elks and moose here. Elks are among the largest deer you'll ever see. You can never mistake a moose for anything else because of its palmate antlers (antlers that look like a hand with the fingers extended outward). They make these deer seem quite distinguished!

Many predatory animals also live in the Rockies. These include coyotes, foxes, grizzly bears and wolverines.

## URAL: THE OLDEST MOUNTAIN RANGE

Many mountains you see on Earth are quite new; they formed only a few million years ago. Yes, that's considered new! But the Urals formed about 300 million years ago! They are believed to be the world's oldest mountain range. Some geologists claim that the Appalachian Mountains, a mountain range in North America, is as old as (or older than) the Urals. The Urals span 2,500 km and cover two countries: Russia and Kazakhstan.

### Hall of Fame: Major Peaks

The Urals are not very tall. The highest mountain of the Urals is Mount Narodnaya, with a height of 1,894 m. The second tallest, Mount Karpinsky, is only a tad bit shorter at 1,878 m.

### Life in the Mountains

You will find many forests and steppes in the Urals. Do you know what steppes are? They are flat areas filled with grass, but not forests. Many animals like wolverines, foxes, brown bears, lynxes and squirrels live in the continental climate. A unique creature is the European polecat—a member of the weasel family. It is very cautious about its territory and marks it with a foul liquid of its own creation! Also, look out for the snowy owl—you might just think Hedwig from Harry Potter is back.

## THE GREAT DIVIDING RANGE: THE LONGEST MOUNTAIN RANGE IN AUSTRALIA

Let's go southwards, shall we? In front of you is the Great Dividing Range, also called the Eastern Highlands. It is the longest mountain range in Australia, covering 3,500 km. But what do these mountains divide? Well, these highlands form a 'watershed'—a land that divides the waters flowing to different oceans. The rivers on the east of these mountains flow toward the Pacific Ocean; those on the west flow toward the lowlands of Australia.

## Hall of Fame: Major Peaks

The tallest peak of this range is that of Mount Kosciuszko. It has a height of 2,228 m. Occupying the second spot is Mount Townsend with a height of 2,209 m.

## Life in the Mountains

It is quite warm in these mountains, with many areas experiencing a tropical or temperate climate. Remember the amazing animals you met on your trip to Australia? You'll find many of them like koalas, kangaroos, wallabies and possums in the mountains. Birds like parrots and kookaburras (kingfishers) are also common.

## THE MID-ATLANTIC RIDGE: THE LONGEST MOUNTAIN RANGE

Do you recall touring the Mid-Atlantic Ridge during your voyage through the Atlantic Ocean? It is a fascinating mountain range as it is (almost) completely underwater! It covers about 16,000 km, making it the longest mountain range on the planet.

This range doesn't run through any country because it is underwater. However, north of the Atlantic Ocean, it separates Europe, Asia and North America. In the south, it separates Africa and South America. Small portions of the range have emerged above water in Iceland and the volcanic islands of Saint Helena and Ascension (part of the British overseas territories).

## Hall of Fame: Major Peaks

Most of the mountains in the Mid-Atlantic Ridge have an average height of 3,000 m. The tallest is Mount Pico in Portugal. It has an elevation of 6,096 m below the sea and 2,350 m above the sea. Now, isn't that impressive?

## Life in the Mountains

Well, what do you think lives near underwater mountains? Many exciting species of planktons, anglerfish and squids!

### EXERCISE 4: HIGHLIGHTS FROM YOUR MOUNTAINEERING TRIP

Did you enjoy scaling the tall mountains and watching the world below diminish in size, just like Alice in *Alice in Wonderland* after she drank the mysterious liquid? Look carefully at the sketches of mountain ranges below and identify them.

1.

Somewhere, hiding in this mountain range, is the cute red panda. Can you name the range?_____

2.

The mountain range shown in this map is the oldest in the world. Name it._____

3.

We'll tell you which mountain range this is: the Eastern Highlands. Can you write down its more common name?_____

4.

The tallest peak in this mountain range is Mount Jindhagada. Which range is it?_____

5.

Don't be scared, but this mountain range is full of volcanoes. Can you identify it?_____

6.

Look closely. Can you see Yellowstone National Park? Write down the name of the mountain range where it belongs._____

7.

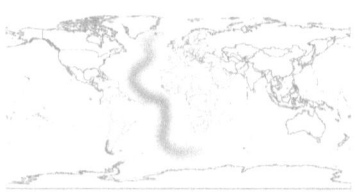

This mountain range is home to the K2! Name it._____

8.

Make sure you don't get wet trying to identify this mountain range, as most of it is under water! Write down its name._____

**9.**

This beautiful mountain range in Europe is home to the ibex, shrew, otter and lynx. Which range is it?_____

**10.**

You can see from the map that this mountain range covers France, Spain and Andorra. What is its name?_____

# RIVERS OF THE WORLD

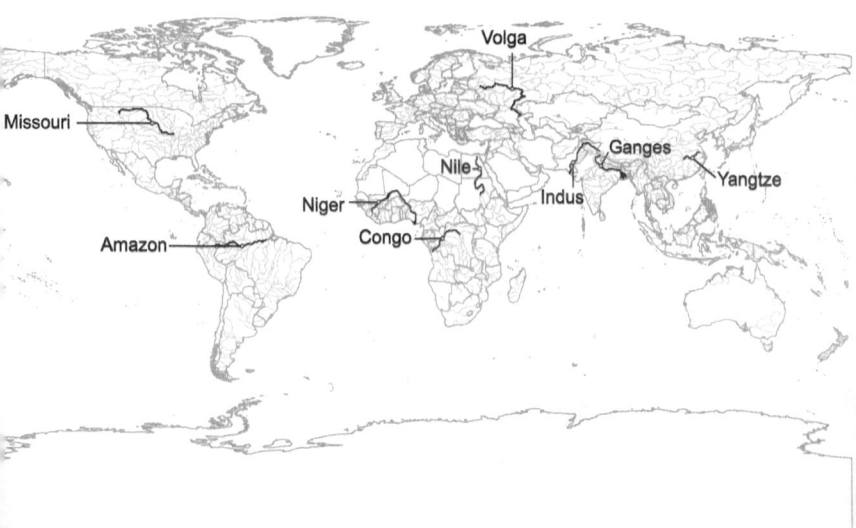

*The world's rivers*

'*Have you got a brook in your little heart, where bashful flowers blow?*' Emily Dickinson wrote this beautiful line about brooks and rivers in her famous poem 'The Brook'. You must have seen flowing bodies of fresh water while you picnicked on the banks, and even fished. These water bodies are called **rivers**. They get their water from springs, glaciers, rainwater, or waterlogged soil.

So, is every freshwater body a river? No. A river must naturally flow towards another river, ocean, sea or lake. You already know about oceans and seas. Lakes (Chapter 11) are inland water bodies surrounded by land. They do not flow like rivers. Streams do flow, but they are usually smaller and shallower than rivers.

A river is joined by many other rivers called **tributaries**. Together, a river and its tributaries drain off their water in the **catchment basin**. Rivers often carry sediments, such as minerals, rocks and plants, with the water. Sometimes sediments get deposited in layers when a river drains off into another waterbody. This pile-up creates a landform called a **delta**. It could be triangular or even resemble a bird's foot.

*A delta*

There are many rivers in the world, and the exact number is hard to determine. Some geologists believe that there are 165 rivers on Earth. Let's cruise down some of the world's most important rivers and unveil their secrets.

## NILE: THE WORLD'S LONGEST RIVER

The Nile is the longest river, not only in Africa, but also in the world. It covers 6,650 km through eleven countries in Africa: Burundi, Democratic Republic of the Congo, Egypt, Eritrea, Ethiopia, Kenya, Rwanda, Sudan, South Sudan, Tanzania and Uganda. The Nile gets its water from the tributaries of lakes Victoria and Tana in Africa, and flows out into the Mediterranean Sea.

The Nile played a significant role in helping the Egyptian civilization bloom in Africa. The river deposited a lot of silt on the banks, making the land fertile. Many areas in Egypt are arid, which is why the banks of the Nile are perfect for habitation and farming. The river used to flood annually, but that stopped after the Egyptians built the Aswan Dam in 1960.

### What Lives in the Water?

Er...things can get very dangerous inside the Nile. Crocodiles, spiders, lizards and mosquitoes are common in these waters. A huge fish called the Nile perch also lives here. It can grow up to 2 m long and weigh as much as 200 kg! The hippopotamuses also enjoy living in the Nile.

One of the most interesting plants growing along the river is the papyrus. The Egyptians used its stem to make paper.

## AMAZON: THE WORLD'S WIDEST RIVER

Hello, you are in another super-long river! The Amazon is the longest river in South America. It covers 6,400 km, which is only a trifle bit shorter than the Nile. But it has a unique record for itself; it is the widest river on Earth, with the largest volume of water.

The Amazon gets its water from glacier-fed lakes in Peru. It flows through six countries in South America: Bolivia, Brazil, Colombia, Ecuador, Peru and Venezuela. Finally, it drains off into the Atlantic Ocean.

## What Lives in the Water?

The Amazon is no less dangerous than the Nile, so remember that before you venture in for a swim. Skulking about in these waters are electric eels and anacondas! Also beware of the bull shark that is very fond of its territory and hates being provoked. Even the little fishes in the Amazon are aggressive. The red-bellied piranha is a fish with immensely sharp teeth that can bite into flesh. Piranhas have frequently attacked human beings.

One of the friendlier creatures in this river is the Amazon river dolphin. Did you know this dolphin changes colour? As it grows old, its colour turns from white to pink!

## GANGES: THE HOLY RIVER

Prepared to take a dip into the holy water of the Ganges, the national river of India? The Ganges spans 2,510 km and is the longest river in India. The Brahmaputra and Indus rivers also flow in India, and are longer. But their territories are not just confined to India, and include Tibet and Pakistan.

The Ganges originates from the Gangotri glacier in the Himalayas. It drains into the Sunderban delta in the Bay of Bengal, most of which extends into Bangladesh. After entering

Bangladesh, the Ganges gets a new name—Padma.

Hindus worship the Ganges as a personification of the Goddess Ganga and believe that bathing here washes away sins. Ironically, the Ganges is also one of the world's most polluted rivers after the Sarno in Italy, the Citarum in Indonesia and the Passaic in the US. It is critical to clean the Ganges as it provides drinking water to the majority of the Indian population.

## What Lives in the Water?

The gharials or crocodiles with bulb-like noses, along with dolphins and otters, love the waters of the Ganges. But the grandest animal living in the Ganges basin is the Bengal tiger! Sadly, its population is dwindling due to habitat destruction by humans.

## CONGO: THE WORLD'S DEEPEST RIVER

Everyone knows that oceans are deep, but surely rivers don't go a long way down? Well, check this out: the Congo river in Africa can go down to depths of 220 m! It is also called the 'Heart of Darkness', as the river meanders like a maze, making it extremely difficult for a swimmer to emerge from it.

The Congo river extends up to 4,700 km. There is so much water in this river that it is the second largest in the world by volume, after the Amazon river. It gets its water from the Lualaba river and Luapula river (both in Africa) and drains into the Atlantic Ocean.

## What Lives in the Water?

Say hello to the manatee or the sea cow! These mammals have

egg-shaped heads, and like cows, mainly eat vegetation. But the trait that most resembles a cow's is its quiet, lazy nature! You can also find otters, crocodiles, tortoises and snakes in the Congo river. Several species of fish also inhabit these deep waters. Watch out for the rather disgusting lungfish that likes to wrap itself in a cocoon of mucus during dry seasons. What can you say, it's a survival strategy!

## YANGTZE: THE WORLD'S BUSIEST RIVER

Since ancient times, rivers have helped humans travel and conduct business. The Yangtze in China is the busiest river in the modern world. It is filled with waterways, with ships transporting bulk goods like coal, and cruise ships carrying passengers. All these human activities have made this river polluted.

The Yangtze river flows across 6,300 km; it is the third longest river on Earth and the longest in Asia. Originating in the Tibetan Plateau, the Yangtze drains off into the South China Sea.

The Three Gorges Dam, which generates hydroelectricity for China, is built on this river. It is the world's largest hydroelectric dam. Sadly, thousands of people had to relocate for the construction of this dam.

### What Lives in the Water?

The increasing pollution has made life in the Yangtze River difficult. Alligators, dolphins, turtles and salamanders live in these waters. The Chinese paddlefish is one of the biggest freshwater fish, lovingly called the 'Giant Panda of the River.' The Yangtze sturgeon is another interesting fish in this river. It looks incredibly bony. Some biologists believe it used to live with the dinosaurs!

## VOLGA: THE LONGEST RIVER IN EUROPE

If the Ganges is sacred for Hindus, the Volga has special meaning for the Russians. The Volga is called 'Mother Volga' in Russia and considered the life-blood of the country. It is a fairly large river spanning 3,530 km in Russia. The Volga originates at the plateaus of the Valdai hills in Russia and drains into the Caspian Sea.

Did you think that the Danube is the longest river in Europe? Well, it isn't. The Danube flows across ten countries: Austria, Bulgaria, Croatia, Hungary, Germany, Moldova, Romania, Serbia, Slovakia and Ukraine. It extends to just 2,860 km. The Danube is, however, the longest river in the European Union (since the EU does not include Russia).

### What Lives in the Water?

The most famous inhabitant of the Volga is the sturgeon. It is a family of twenty-seven different species of fish that usually grow to be quite long, even extending up to 3.6 m. Sturgeon eggs are used to make a delicacy called 'caviar' that is very popular across the world.

In this river, you might also meet the little Russian desman, which looks like a small mole. Caspian seals like living here too!

## MISSOURI: THE LONGEST RIVER IN NORTH AMERICA

Look out! You're in the 'Big Muddy'! The Missouri river, the longest river in North America, is notorious for carrying too much sediment, giving it a rather muddy sobriquet. It covers 3,726 km and flows across two countries: the US and Canada.

The Missouri originates from three other rivers in the United States: the Jefferson, the Gallatin and the Madison. It takes the water from the confluence of these rivers and drains it into the Mississippi river. The Mississippi river was once believed to be the longest river in North America. Some geologists club the two and call it the Mississippi-Missouri river.

## What Lives in the Water?

Your friend—the sturgeon—lives in the Missouri River too. This species is called the pallid sturgeon. Unfortunately, it is now endangered due to habitat destruction. Frogs, toads and snakes also make themselves at home in the Missouri.

Three species of endangered migratory birds adore this river: the piping plover, the interior tern and the American bald eagle. These birds find the river area very useful for breeding and feeding, especially in the winters.

## EXERCISE 5: HIGHLIGHTS FROM YOUR CROSS-RIVER CRUISE

Watch out! Don't soak the paper with droplets from your river cruise! The map below shows the location of some of the major rivers on Earth. Write down the name of the river corresponding to its number in the space provided below. Also, write the name of the basin/outlet of each river.

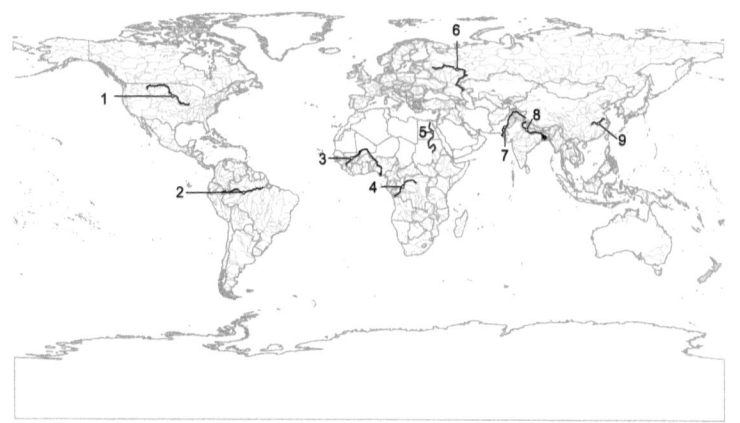

1. _____
2. _____
3. _____
4. _____
5. _____
6. _____
7. _____
8. _____
9. _____

# FORESTS OF THE WORLD

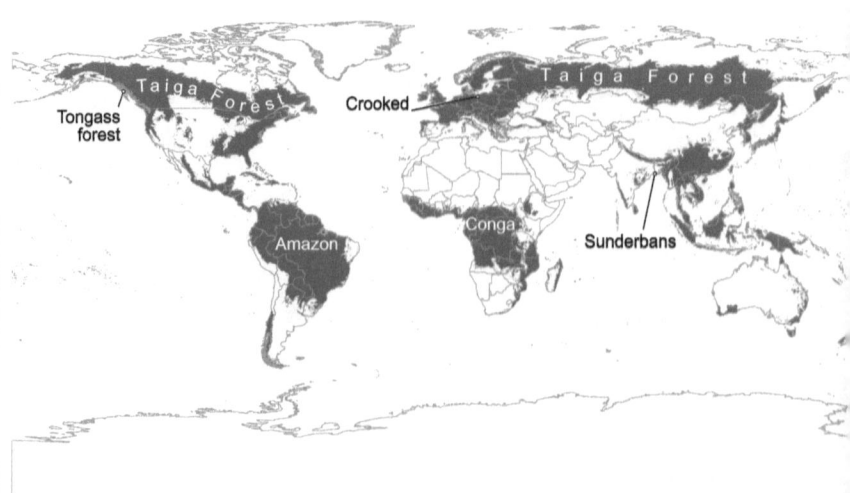

*World's biggest forests*

Have you ever been to a forest? It can be scary to be among dense foliage and wild beasts, but it's also beautiful. **Forests** are huge areas of land, full of trees and undergrowth. While it is impossible to count the exact number of forests on Earth, it is known that they cover almost one-third of the planet. Thank God for that, because forests supply us with oxygen to breathe! And they are home to most of our flora and fauna. However, as we cut down more and more trees, the planet's forest cover decreases dangerously.

There are broadly three kinds of forests depending on their latitudinal location: **tropical** (equator), **temperate** (middle latitudes) and **boreal** (sub-Arctic).

Tropical forests are warm and wet with temperatures around 27°C. They grow in South America, Africa and Southeast Asia. These forests teem with plants and animals.

Temperate forests grow in North America, Europe and Northeast Asia. They have a wide range of temperature (-30°C to 30°C) and four distinct seasons of summer, winter, spring and autumn.

Boreal forests have bitterly cold winters and short warmer summers. Temperatures range from -40°C to 20°C. They grow in Alaska, Canada, Siberia and Scandinavia.

Pack your bag of essentials, including night-vision glasses, for we will now embark on a journey into some of the world's largest and most mysterious forests!

## TAIGA OR BOREAL FOREST: THE LARGEST FOREST IN THE WORLD

Welcome to a jumbo forest that covers 29 per cent of the world's entire forest area on its own! This forest spans over three continents: Europe, Asia and North America. It stretches through ten countries: Canada, Finland, Iceland, Japan, Mongolia, Norway, Russia, Sweden, Scotland and the United States.

The Taiga is so enormous that it undoubtedly has a great range of temperature. You can expect it to be as cold as -50°C and as warm as 30°C! It doesn't rain much here, but it snows. These forests have many coniferous evergreen trees like spruce, pine, fir and cedar. These trees grow in the form of a canopy to get as much of the limited sunlight as possible. Small plants like mosses and berries grow under these thick canopies.

What about the animals? Only those who love winters—like the wolverines, elks, lynxes, bears, reindeers and wolves—can live in the Taiga. Sometimes migratory birds fly over to breed, while others like sparrows and finches permanently live here.

## Fire in the Forest

Do you know fires are very common in the Taiga? These wildfires are nature's way of ensuring that the thick canopy burns from time to time to let small plants grow on the ground. That's how the little herbivorous animals in the forest get their food.

## TONGASS NATIONAL FOREST, ALASKA: THE WORLD'S OLDEST FOREST

How long do you think trees live? Thirty, forty or seventy years? Well, some trees in the Tongass National Forest have been around for more than 800 years! This forest spreads across Southeast Alaska and is among the largest temperate rainforests in the world.

It is cold in the Tongass. Temperatures rarely go above 4-15°C although some 'extremely warm' temperatures like 26°C have been recorded. It rains quite a bit, so raingear is essential!

Growing abundantly in this forest are coniferous trees like spruce and hemlock. Hemlock trees are the most common trees in all of Alaska.

Living in the depths of the Tongass are several interesting animals. Watch out for the Sitka black-tailed deer and the grizzly bear. Their sightings are widespread. The marbled murrelet also loves this forest. It is a small cute little seabird whose population has severely dwindled. Other birds that enjoy the Tongass are bald eagles and a predatory bird called the northern goshawk. We can all learn a lesson or two about persistence from the northern goshawk. It is such a determined bird that it can chase its prey for more than forty-five minutes!

## AMAZON RAINFOREST: THE WORLD'S MOST DANGEROUS FOREST

Be warned before you enter the largest rainforest in the world— it is not safe in there. Wild animals roam about free; it is crazily humid and hot, and you're unlikely to escape from being bitten by mosquitoes. This forest is the largest in South America and covers eight countries: Bolivia, Brazil, Colombia, Ecuador, Guyana, Peru, Suriname and Venezuela. It also covers French Guiana—a French territory in South America.

It gets really wet and warm here. The temperature ranges between 18–22°C. It keeps raining here, with some areas getting as much as 430 inches of rain. This is in contrast to India that only gets an average of 25 inches of rain annually! Do be careful of 'The Friaje'. It is a climatic phenomenon that happens between June and November. Cool winds from the Andes lower the temperature to 5°C!

Geologists don't know all the species of plants, animals and insects that live in these forests. But you can see rubber trees, mahogany and cocoa trees. Dangerous animals like the terrifying anaconda, a crocodile called 'caiman', jaguars and poison dart frogs live here. Lazy sloths hang from tree branches. Kingfishers, vultures and spectacled owls fly about overhead. Many tribal communities also live in these forests, several of them 'uncontacted' and secretive.

## CONGO BASIN FOREST: THE SECOND LARGEST TROPICAL FOREST

Don't abandon your water bottles yet, for you're in the Earth's second largest tropical forest. The Congo Basin Forest is Africa's largest forest and it covers nine countries: Angola, Burundi, Cameroon, Central African Republic, Democratic Republic of the Congo, Republic of the Congo, Rwanda, Tanzania and Zambia.

As you'd expect in rainforests, the climate is hot and humid. The average temperature is 25°C. However, it doesn't rain as much as it does in the Amazon forests. The annual rainfall averages at 1.47 m (58 inches).

If you like monkeys, you'll love this forest! It is home to gorillas, bonobos and chimpanzees. Do you know that bonobos are among our closest relatives? They share 98.7 per cent of their DNA (genetic material) with humans! Bonobos look just like chimpanzees, except they're shorter and darker. African forest elephants are also among the residents of the Congo Basin Forest. They like to live deep inside the forest. Do you know how officials estimate their population? Through 'dung count' or the analysis of their faeces on the ground!

Many endemic plants grow in this forest, i.e. plants that you'll only find in this region. Okoumé trees are very popular for their timber. However, too much human activity in the forest is never healthy for its biodiversity.

## CROOKED FOREST, POLAND: THE 'TWISTED' FOREST

Have you ever seen a ghost? While spooks may or may not exist, you might just get a fright amidst the crooked pine trees in Poland's famous forest. It is among the largest and most mysterious forests in Europe, filled with oddly-shaped trees that resemble the letter 'J'! Some people believe that the trees were crushed by tanks during the Second World War (1939–1945) which made them grow curved. Others think aliens did it.

The Crooked Forest is one of the most fascinating forests in Europe—a small continent that has the maximum forested area on Earth. Sweden has so many forests that they cover almost 69 per cent of the total area! If you want to explore a truly haunted forest, visit the Black Forest in Germany. People claim to have seen a headless horseman, riding on his big white horse. Yikes!

It can get quite cold in the Crooked Forest, with temperatures dipping below the freezing point, and trees getting snow-capped in the winters. Wonder if the ghosts mind the cold—what do you think?

Not many large wild animals live in this forest, but you can get friendly with cheerful rabbits, timid squirrels and screeching owls. These animals don't mind that the trees are crooked, as long as they can play amidst the branches!

## SUNDERBANS, INDIA: THE LAND OF THE BENGAL TIGER

Prepare to come face-to-face with the majestic Bengal tiger, famous all over the world for its gorgeous black stripes, large canine teeth and long claws suited for climbing trees. The Sunderbans in India and Bangladesh is the only forest where the Bengal tiger is found. This forest is full of mangrove trees and wet areas. Mangroves are small shrub-like trees that grow in swampy, saline water. The Sunderbans is among the world's largest mangrove belts.

It is hot and humid here, with temperatures ranging from 20°C to over 40°C. The humidity is over 80 per cent, which means you will always need a gigantic umbrella! It's a good idea to visit during winters (October to February) when it's cooler and drier. The Bengal tiger is undoubtedly the celebrity of the Sunderbans. But its population is being threatened by human activity. The Sunderbans is also home to leopards, crocodiles and panthers.

## EXERCISE 6: HIGHLIGHTS FROM YOUR JUNGLE SAFARI

If you survived from being eaten by a wild animal in the forest, welcome back! Recap your forest experiences by answering the questions below.

1.

The region shown on the map seems to be covered with this forest! Write down the name of the forest and the continent where it is located._____

2.

Look at all those bonobos jumping about on the map! Can't see them? Well, tell us the name of the forest and the continent, and you just might!_____

3.

The forest shown in this map has a humidity of over 80 per cent. What is it called and in which continent is it located? _____

4.

Something is spooky about both the forests on the upper part of this map. If you aren't scared of ghosts, can you write down the names of these forests and the continent to which they belong?_____

5.

The northern goshawk is often seen in the forest shown on the map (the shaded area on the left). Do you know the name of the forest and the continent?_____

6.

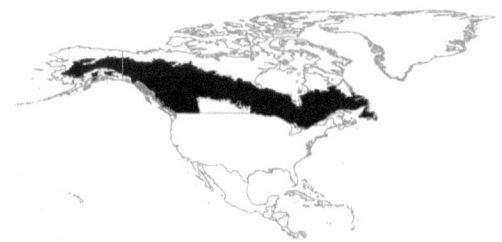

Look at this jumbo forest; it covers three continents! This map shows only a part of it. Can you name the forest and the continents it covers?_____

# DESERTS OF THE WORLD

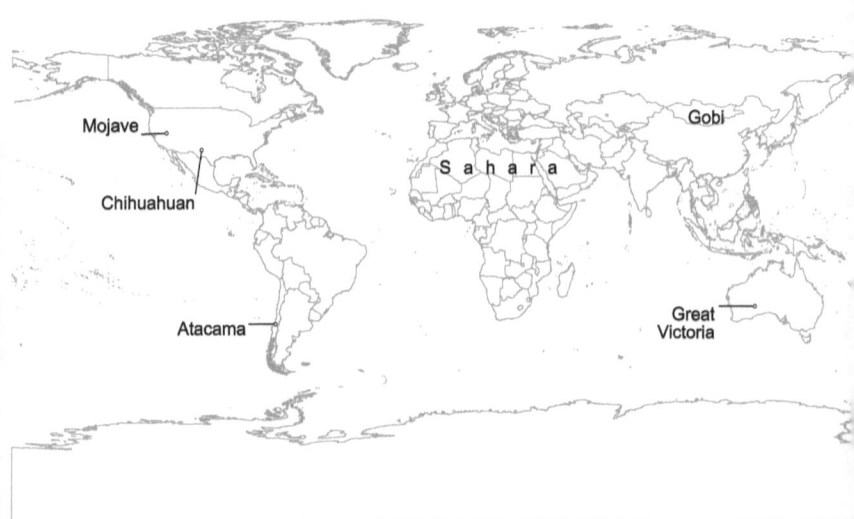

*World's biggest deserts*

What comes to your mind when someone says, 'desert'? Large stretches of sand, camels, a hot sun, and hardly any rain? Well, not all deserts are blazing hot, but they are definitely dry. A **desert** is an area that receives less than 250 mm of annual rainfall (less than ten inches). Almost a third of the Earth is covered by deserts! Some people believe there are thirty-three major deserts in the world, and seventy-one if you count the smaller ones. But in reality, it is a difficult count.

You can find deserts in every continent except Europe. While the largest desert is the entire continent of Antarctica, the smallest is the Carcross Desert in Canada, which occupies only 2.6 sq km. So, how come there aren't any deserts in Europe? Well, there are definitely dry areas such as Tabernas in Spain, but most of the continent gets enough rainfall to not allow a desert to develop.

There are four types of deserts on Earth:

**Polar deserts** that are cold throughout the year

**Subtropical deserts** that are always hot

**Cold winter deserts** that have dry summers, but get some rainfall during winter

**Coastal deserts** that have cool winters and hot summers.

Are you prepared for some extreme weather? Let's begin our journey through some of the fascinating deserts of the world.

## THE SAHARA DESERT: THE LARGEST DESERT IN AFRICA

Welcome to the quintessential desert landscape of dunes, dry valleys and large stretches with no plants, animals or human beings! The Sahara Desert is the third largest desert in the world, after the Antarctic and Arctic deserts. It covers 9.4 million sq km—this is about 10 per cent of the Earth's total area. It is located entirely in Africa, covering ten countries: Algeria, Chad, Egypt, Libya, Mali, Mauritania, Morocco, Niger, Sudan and Tunisia. The Sahara is bordered by the Red Sea and the Mediterranean Sea.

It is blazing hot here. While the average temperature is around 30°C, it can easily cross 50°C during summer. Can you guess the highest temperature recorded here? It was 58°C in Aziziyah, Libya—not something your regular air conditioner can help with!

Who can survive in such a hot desert? Hardly any plants live here other than the resilient 'halophytes'. Halophytes are shrub-like desert plants that have adapted to saline conditions. However, some animals such as hyenas, monitor lizards, vipers, dung beetles and gerbils (that resemble desert rats) have embraced the Sahara desert.

So, is it going to be a walk amidst the dunes all the time? Not at all! The Sahara desert has several mountain peaks, the highest of which is the Emi Koussi—a volcanic peak with a height of 3,415 m.

## THE MOJAVE DESERT: THE HOTTEST DESERT IN THE WORLD

On a day in July in the year 1913, a temperature of 56.7°C was recorded in an area called Furnace Creek Ranch, in Death Valley. Morbidly named thus because of these insanely high temperatures, the Death Valley region makes the Mojave Desert in North America the hottest in the world. It isn't a large desert, as it only covers 1,24,000 sq km and lies entirely in the US, that too mostly in the state of California.

### What is the Hottest Temperature Ever Recorded on Earth?

Is 56.7°C the hottest temperature ever recorded on Earth? No, the hottest our planet has seen is 70.7°C in the Lut Desert of

Iran. Wait a moment—then why isn't Lut Desert considered the hottest? It is because this temperature reading was done by a satellite and not a ground thermometer. Satellite readings are considered less accurate.

It can get sweltering in Mojave during the day and bitterly cold during the night. Not many plants and animals can survive in such a climate. The beavertail cactus, barrel cactus and desert candle are some of the common plants found here. The Mojave is also home to lizards, toads, owls, foxes and mule deer. During your trip, watch out for the 'ghost towns'. Ghost towns are areas where people once lived, but have now been abandoned.

## THE GOBI DESERT: THE LARGEST DESERT IN ASIA

Do you know the meaning of 'gobi'? It is the Mongolian word for a place without any water. The Gobi Desert is among the world's greatest deserts, measuring 1.295 million sq km in area. It covers large tracts of land in Mongolia and China, and is bordered by the Tian Shan mountain range and the Niu Bei mountain.

The weather in the Gobi desert is extreme. It can get as cold as −40°C in the winter and as hot as 45°C in the summer. Due to such fluctuations, few plants survive. You can occasionally find succulent grass, potash bushes and yellowwood bean capers. Camels, gazelles, antelopes and marmots (a large squirrel) roam around the sandy but rocky landscape. The Bactrian camel is sure to catch your eye because of its two humps. This gives it an unusual appearance when compared to the 'dromedary camel' found in the Sahara Desert that has only one hump.

Millions of years ago, dinosaurs also lived in the Gobi desert. Scientists have found dinosaur fossils from the Mesozoic Era (252–66 million years ago). Wonder where they all went, don't you?

Did you know that the Gobi desert hides luxurious secrets under its sands? It is home to Oyu Tolgoi—the third largest copper and gold mine in the world!

## THE CHIHUAHUAN DESERT: THE LARGEST NORTH AMERICAN DESERT

Do you find the cactus plant fascinating? So full of thorns and reserves of water in its body, the cactus is quite interesting. It is widespread, with over 300 species of plants in the Chihuahuan Desert, the largest desert in North America covering 362,600 sq km in the US and Mexico. Many Mexican people also use the cactus for treating arthritis.

This desert is located at a height of about 914–1524 m, which makes nights and winters quite cold. But during the day, the temperature can reach up to 40°C.

The Chihuahuan desert is also interesting because a river called the Rio Grande runs right through it! Many animals live here because of this, including deer, foxes, antelopes, snakes and lizards. Plant life, however, is limited to shrubs of different kinds. You can find yuccas, agaves and prickly pears.

But wait—if a river runs through it, how is it a desert? The Chihuahuan is a 'rain shadow' desert, which means it is situated on that side of a mountain range that doesn't receive rainfall. On either side of this desert are two mountain ranges—the Sierra Madre Occidental and the Sierra Madre

Oriental. They prevent any moisture from reaching the desert.

## THE ATACAMA DESERT: THE WORLD'S DRIEST DESERT

It doesn't rain much in deserts; that's why they are called deserts, right? But the Atacama desert in South America, that spans Chile, Bolivia, Peru and Argentina, has it particularly rough. It is the driest desert in the world with an average annual rainfall of less than 1 mm (0.04 inches)! This desert is the largest in South America, covering almost 105,000 sq km, lying mostly to the west of the Andes.

The Atacama experiences major weather fluctuations every day. It can get as hot as 40°C in the daytime, and go down to 5°C at night. You may be wearing sleeveless tees in the day but will shiver inside layers of quilts at bedtime!

Hardly any plants and animals live in this unfriendly desert. You can occasionally spot lizards, foxes and mice. Some plants that somehow manage to survive are algae, lichens and cacti.

Would you believe that countries actually fought a war to work in a desert with such a climate? It is true! In the years 1879-83, Bolivia, Chile and Peru fought the **War of the Pacific** to decide who would control the massive reserves of sodium nitrate in the Atacama desert. This is a chemical compound used to make fertilizers and explosives.

## THE GREAT VICTORIA: THE BIGGEST DESERT IN AUSTRALIA

The land Down Under might be an island, but it isn't devoid of deserts. The Great Victoria is Australia's largest desert at 348,750 sq km, and it has a typically arid landscape with dunes, stony plains and only some shallow lakes. It surely has a regal name, doesn't it? The desert was named after Queen Victoria, the former queen of the UK. It was Ernest Giles, an Australian explorer, and the first to cross the desert with his team, who gave it this name.

It is moderately hot during summer with temperatures crossing 32°C. In the winter, it gets reasonably cool, at about 18°C. Doesn't really sound like desert temperature, does it? But the rainfall here is low and unreliable. This is what makes the area much more arid than it may have been otherwise.

The Great Victoria Desert houses many threatened species of birds. Watch out for the princess parrot, the scarlet-chested parrot, and the mallee fowl. Like her home, the princess parrot also has royal connections; she was named after the Princess Alexandra of Denmark, who later became the queen of the UK. Some of the animals you will see here are wallabies, lizards and snakes. Interestingly enough for a desert, you will also find many colourful plants and flowers like marble gum, black oak and acacia.

## EXERCISE 7: HIGHLIGHTS FROM YOUR DESERT ADVENTURE

We bet you are thirsty after that exhausting trip across the world's deserts. Go and get a drink of water. Now study the map below and write down the names of the deserts that are marked with an arrow across various continents.

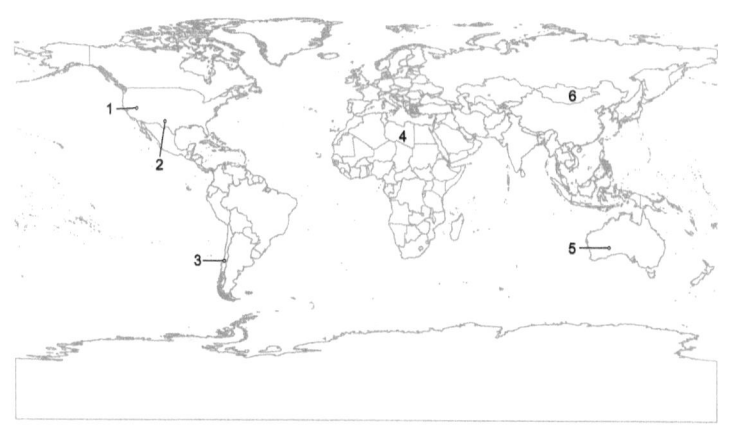

1. _____

2. _____

3. _____

4. _____

5. _____

6. _____

# ISLANDS OF THE WORLD

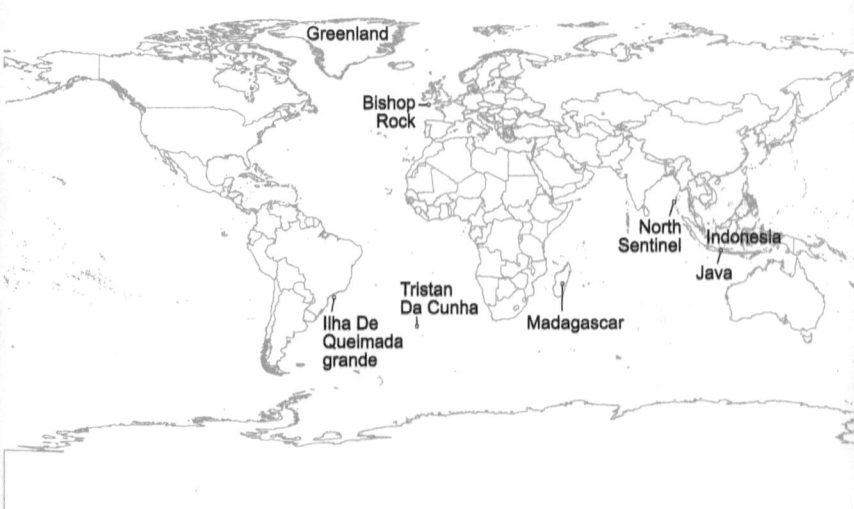

*World's most popular islands*

Have you ever visited Kirrin Island with George, Timmy and the rest of the *Famous Five*? The renowned author Enid Blyton created a captivating island world with old castles, jackdaws, cliffs and the blue, blue sea. **Islands** are areas of land surrounded by water (ocean, sea, river or lake), and have always attracted tourists. Do you remember that continents are also surrounded by water? But they are too huge to be called islands.

Sometimes, many islands are located together in the same

area. They are called an **archipelago.** No one knows for sure how many islands are there in the world, but it is estimated that there are thousands. Some islands are so small—less than 0.0636 km in area—that they are called **islets**. Cute name, isn't it?

Depending on how they were formed, there are six main types of islands in the world:

**Continental islands** are believed to have broken off and drifted away from larger continents. Madagascar is a continental island in the Indian Ocean. Have you seen the famous animation movie named after the island? In the real world too, it is home to hundreds of animals and birds!

**Tidal islands** are also continental, but the land that connects the island to the mainland goes underwater at high tide. The Mont Saint-Michel Island in France is a tidal island.

**Barrier islands** lie between the ocean and the mainland. Many of them were formed by glaciers. Did you know that New York is also a barrier island?

**Oceanic islands** are formed when volcanoes present on the ocean floor erupt. Japan has many such islands. Be careful!

**Coral islands** are built by sea animals called corals. These fascinating creatures have hard skeletons made of calcium carbonate. The Bahamas are coral islands.

**Artificial islands** are man-made for housing and other purposes. But how can you make an island? Countries do it by expanding an existing islet and filling the area with cement, rock and other material. It is called 'land reclamation'. Dubai has many such island complexes.

Are you all set for island-hopping and exploring the beautiful landscapes that have long attracted travellers? Let's go!

## GREENLAND: THE WORLD'S LARGEST ISLAND

About 50,000 people live on the entire island of Greenland, over an area of 2,166,086 sq km. Do you know what that implies? As of 2018, only about 0.026 people lived per square kilometre—that's not even one!

The frigid weather of Greenland makes it the least densely populated country in the world. Located close to North America, Greenland is an autonomous territory of Denmark. So, even though the Queen of Denmark rules Greenland, they do have their own prime minister. The capital city is Nuuk.

You can find glaciers all over Greenland. Many of these glaciers keep producing icebergs. Guess which animals love this kind of climate—polar bears, reindeer and seals! Much of the traditional food in Greenland is also based on meat from marine animals. If you like seafood, you should definitely taste 'suaasat'. It comprises meat from seals, reindeers and birds, flavoured with pepper, onions and all things nice! Yum!

There are many other huge islands in the world other than Greenland. New Guinea and Borneo are the second and the third largest islands respectively, and both of them are in Southeast Asia. There are also some places on Earth you'd never have guessed are islands, like Britain and Japan!

## BISHOP ROCK: THE WORLD'S SMALLEST ISLAND

Is it a rock or is it an island? Geologists differ in their opinions, but most people agree that Bishop Rock in the Atlantic Ocean is the world's smallest island. It is located in the Cornwall region of the UK. It is tinier than the tiny islands you must have dreamt of. It is 46 m long and 16 m wide.

On the island is a large lighthouse where many tourists go every year. Before the lighthouse was built, many ships got wrecked when they hit the island in the darkness at night. Thank God for the reassuring lighthouse that has been in operation since 1858! Before that, lighthouse keepers used to stay there and operate it using candles and paraffin vapour lamps, but now the service has been automated. You can even stay inside the tower for a couple of weeks. Wouldn't that be super-duper exciting?

There are several other little islands on Earth, many of which are inhabited. The Sea Lion Island in the South Atlantic Ocean, which is close to South America, is about 9.05 sq km in area. Only a handful of people live here, but tourists can stay in a lodge and converse with lots of penguins and seals. An island on the Saint Lawrence river of New York is recognized as the smallest inhabited island. It has enough space only for a house and a tree owned by the Sizelands family. Wonder if they ever get lonely!

## TRISTAN DA CUNHA: THE REMOTEST ISLAND IN THE WORLD

Do you sometimes wish to explore places so distant that no one can disturb you? The island of Tristan da Cunha in the

Atlantic Ocean is the world's remotest island where people still live. It covers an area of 207 sq km and has a population of 250 people. Tristan da Cunha is an overseas territory of Britain, located between South Africa and South America.

So, why is it called the remotest inhabited island in the world? Well, the nearest city from the island is Cape Town in South Africa. Do you know how long it takes to travel from the island to Cape Town? Seven days by boat! You cannot go by air because there are no airports on this island.

On the middle of this island is a giant volcano. It has a height of 2,060 m. If the volcano erupts—as it did in 1961—the people of the island will have no choice but to escape by boat or be evacuated!

Are there other remote, far-off islands like Tristan da Cunha? The Kerguelen Islands in the Indian Ocean is also extremely remote. It is almost 3,300 km from Madagascar, the nearest inhabited location. Only about a hundred people live here; most of them are scientists and researchers.

## ILHA DA QUEIMADA GRANDE: THE MOST DANGEROUS ISLAND EVER

Can you guess what the name of this island means? Snake Island! You can now imagine why the Ilha da Queimada Grande island in Brazil is considered the most dangerous in the world.

This island is a minuscule piece of land in Brazil with an area of 0.43 sq km. Zoologists believe there are five venomous snakes every 0.09 sq m, ready to attack anyone who sets foot on their territory! The golden lancehead pit viper—an endangered poisonous snake—lives here, feeding on birds. So, why does this island have so many snakes? They were trapped when the sea level rose many years ago, unable to return to the mainland.

Earth has many more dangerous islands. Some are naturally unsafe like the island of Saba in the Netherlands (hurricanes) or the Ramree Island in Burma (crocodiles). But some have become lethal due to human activities. No one can live on the Marshall Islands in the Pacific Ocean, due to the radioactive dumping by the US government.

Sometimes it is the people on the island who are dangerous. The North Sentinel Island, which is part of India's Andaman and Nicobar islands, has tribal people who have no connection with the outside world. There have been reports that when helicopters tried to land on the island, the tribals inhabiting the island threw stones and shot arrows at the visitors!

## JAVA: THE ISLAND WITH THE MAXIMUM PEOPLE

If you think islands are either idyllic or dangerous, prepare to be overwhelmed by your visit to the island of Java in Indonesia. It is the world's most populated island with over 141,370,000 people. That is almost as much as the population of England! Java is home to more than 50 per cent of Indonesia's population. Jakarta, the capital of Indonesia, is also a part of Java.

Java experiences a hot, tropical climate. The average temperature ranges from 22°C to 29°C. It rarely gets cold, so you should keep your summer clothing with you at all times.

Have you seen 'Java' drinks in cafes, most of them coffee-based? Back in the seventeenth century, when Indonesia was colonized by the Dutch, many coffee plants were set up here.

The coffee from this region got so famous that Java is now a synonym for coffee!

## Look, a Crowd on the Island!

Many islands on Earth are overcrowded, and a lot of them are in Indonesia. Sumatra, an island in Indonesia, has 50,180,000 people. Borneo, an island shared by Brunei, Indonesia and Malaysia, has 21,258,000 people. Borneo is famous for its ancient rainforest, which is believed to be 130 million years old. Japan and Great Britain are also among the most crowded islands in the world.

### THE TOURIST FAVOURITES

We saved the best for the last—the breathtaking islands with marvellous views! Thousands of tourists visit these islands for annual vacations with their families and friends.

**The Maldives** in the Indian Ocean is among the most popular islands, known for its aquamarine beaches and white shores. You'll find coral reefs under the clear waters while you enjoy snorkelling and scuba diving. The Maldives is an archipelago with 26 atolls. Atolls are coral islands that completely or partly encircle a lagoon (a stretch of salt water separated from the sea).

The island of **Santorini** in Greece is extremely popular for its blue-dome churches and European-style white houses. Make sure you visit the two most famous spots: Firá and Oia.

For a cultural extravaganza, the island of **Bali** in Indonesia is a must visit. It is a green country full of Hindu temples.

A famous tourist island in the continent of Australia is **Fiji,** renowned for its palm trees, friendly people and turquoise waters.

If you want to waddle along with turtles and rays in the clear-blue water of a lagoon, the island of **Bora Bora** in French Polynesia (between South America and Australia) is astounding. It is a lovely tourist spot for luxurious holidays with diving, snorkelling and delicious food.

## EXERCISE 8: HIGHLIGHTS FROM YOUR ISLAND-HOPPING TRIP

Welcome back from your mega-voyage across the islands of the world. Let's review your trip with a few questions.

1.

See that lonely island circled in the ocean on the map somewhat midway between South America and Africa? It has been circled so that you can spot it easily. It has a large volcano right in the middle of it! Which island and ocean are these?

_____

**2.**

There are many famous islands in Southeast Asia as shown on the map. Can you name four?

B_ _ _
_U_A_ _A
B_ _ _ E_
_A_A

**3.**

The island shown on the map is full of glaciers. Write down its name and capital._____

**4.**

Do you recognize the country on the map? The world's newest island formed near it some years ago. Name the island and the country._____

5.

The people on this island on the right of India's map don't seem to like others! Can you guess which island this is and in which country it is located?_____

6.

A continental island in this ocean has a movie named after it. Can you name the island and the ocean?_____

# VOLCANOES OF THE WORLD

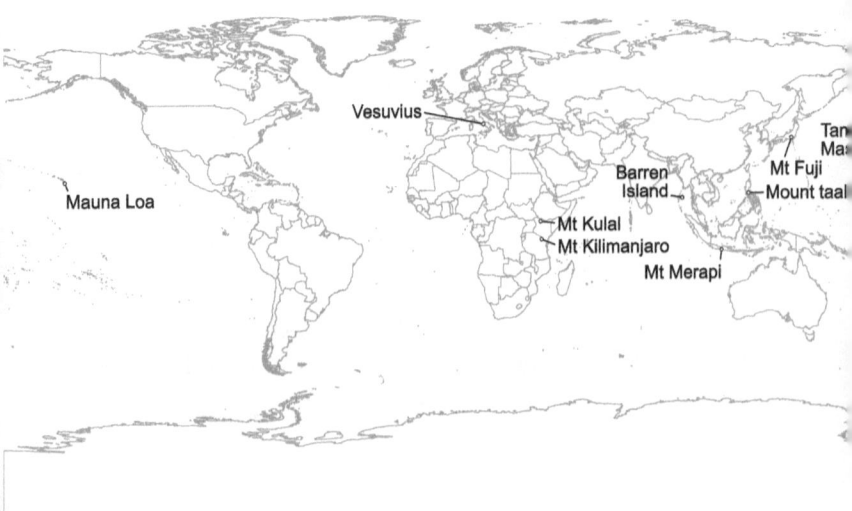

*World's most famous volcanoes*

Have you ever made a live model of a volcano for a school project? There is something riveting about a **volcano**—an opening on the Earth's surface that seems to spew out a red-hot, molten substance from deep down. This erupted material is called **magma** when it's underground and **lava** after it reaches the surface. It consists of minerals, rocks, and dissolved gases.

So, why do volcanoes erupt? This happens when the Earth's

tectonic plates move apart. The magma rises from deep within to fill the space. Sometimes volcanoes erupt when tectonic plates move toward each other, pushing down the Earth's crust. The resulting heat and pressure makes the magma rise and erupt.

Volcanoes are of three types:

- **Active volcanoes** with recent eruptions, like Santa Maria in Guatemala.
- **Dormant volcanoes** that may erupt in the future, like Mount Edziza in Canada.
- **Extinct volcanoes** that won't erupt again, like Mount Kulal in Kenya.

Some geologists claim there are 1,500 active volcanoes on Earth that have exploded in the past. The 'Ring of Fire' in the Pacific Ocean has the maximum number of volcanoes in one place. It has 452 volcanoes deep under America, Japan and Indonesia! Are you sure you aren't scared? Let's get started on our journey through some of the most interesting volcanoes on our planet.

## TAMU MASSIF: THE WORLD'S LARGEST VOLCANO

Tamu Massif is a colossal volcano measuring 292,500 sq km in area. And yet you might never be able to see it. Surprised? Well, the largest volcano on Earth, located close to Japan, is mostly hidden under the ocean. It is believed to have erupted catastrophically several years ago, but is now extinct.

The Tamu Massif is the tallest mountain in the Shatsky Rise—an underwater mountain formed over 130 million years ago. Geologists call it a 'shield volcano', a volcanic mountain built purely out of lava.

For a long time, the Tamu Massif wasn't considered the largest volcano, as geologists thought it wasn't a single volcano but a combination of many. **Mauna Loa** (meaning 'Long Mountain') in Hawaii was considered the largest volcano. Remember how we journeyed to Mount Everest, the tallest mountain on Earth? When you measure from the foot of the mountain and not the sea level, Mauna Loa is the *real* winner. It easily becomes the tallest mountain with a height of 17,000 m, beating the 8,848-metre high Mount Everest.

The Mauna Loa has erupted more than thirty times in history, with its last eruption in 1984. At 48 km long, this active volcano makes up almost half of the island of Hawaii.

## TAAL VOLCANO: THE WORLD'S SMALLEST ACTIVE VOLCANO

You wouldn't think that something as fiery as a volcano could be situated in the middle of a lake. But the Taal Volcano, the smallest active volcano on Earth, is located in the beautiful Taal Lake in the Philippines. It is 508 m tall. Compare this with the Eiffel Tower in Paris that's 324 m tall.

The Taal Volcano is very active. It has erupted almost thirty-three times in the past—the last time in 1977—killing nearly 6000 people. You never know when it might burst again; watch out!

Did you know that the Taal Volcano did not have the title of the world's smallest volcano for a long time? People gave that title to **Cuexcomate** in Mexico. It is only 13 m tall with a diameter of 23 m. That is almost the size of a house!

But geologists have since discovered that Cuexcomate isn't a volcano at all, but only a geyser. It was formed thousands of years ago after the eruption of the Popocatépetl, an active volcano in Mexico. When that volcano erupted, it triggered a geothermal spring circulation under the Earth, giving birth to the geyser.

Did you know that you can even take a staircase right down to the depths of the Cuexcomate? There's nothing to be afraid of; the geyser is now inactive and highly unlikely to ever throw hot water at you again.

## MOUNT VESUVIUS: THE MOST DANGEROUS VOLCANO ON EARTH

What would you say about a volcano that annihilated two entire cities, burying hundreds of people under the lava? Mount Vesuvius in Italy is the only active volcano in Europe, but is the most dangerous one on Earth! One of its most destructive explosions was in AD 79, when it buried the Roman cities of Pompeii and Herculaneum. Today, tourists visit these two ancient cities preserved under the lava that has now receded. In 1631, Vesuvius erupted again and killed 4,000 people! The volcano is gigantic, with a height of 1,281 m.

Even though Mount Vesuvius hasn't erupted since 1944, it is lying in wait, ready to explode at any time. The Italian government has prepared detailed plans to rescue the thousands of people who live near this dangerous giant in case it erupts. If Vesuvius erupts in its full rage today, it could destroy the Italian city of Naples.

## Why Do People Live Near a Volcano?

Wait—if the volcano is so dangerous, why do people live near it? Well, thanks to the volcano, the soil in the area is wonderful for agriculture. The lava releases essential nutrients into the soil, making it highly fertile. The farm produce grown in the vicinity of Mount Vesuvius, such as tomatoes and citrus fruits, are among the best in Italy.

## DANGER LURKS HERE: THE SCARIEST ACTIVE VOLCANOES ON EARTH

While travelling around our planet, don't forget to be mindful of the dangerous active volcanoes that abound! While California and Japan are notorious for witnessing more volcanic eruptions than anywhere else, you can find active volcanoes in Africa (**Erta Ale** in Ethiopia), Alaska (**Mount Cleveland**) and even in Antarctica (**Mount Erebus**)!

**Mount Merapi** in Indonesia keeps blowing smoke from its top several days of the year. It erupted as recently as May 2018, prompting the government to evacuate people. No wonder the name of this volcano means 'fire mountain'!

**Sakurajima** in Japan is the country's most active volcano. Would you believe it used to be an island? One fine day, it started spewing out lava and has been erupting now and then ever since!

Another dangerous volcano in Italy—as if Mount Vesuvius wasn't enough—is **Mount Stromboli**. It is located near Sicily and has been erupting continuously for hundreds of years. Do you want to taste some red-hot stromboli? Don't panic; we meant the famous Italian dough made with cheese, cold cuts and vegetables.

On your island trip to Andaman and Nicobar, you can visit the only active volcano in India—**Barren Island**. It last erupted as recently as January 2017!

## SLEEPIEST VOLCANOES: THE EARTH'S MOST DORMANT VOLCANOES

Everyone needs to take a break sometimes, even volcanoes. When volcanoes go several years without an eruption, geologists say they are sleeping or 'dormant'. A dormant volcano can, at any time, turn into an active one that spews out lava!

The **Mauna Kea** in Hawaii is a dormant volcano that hasn't erupted since 2460 BC. Mauna Kea means 'white mountain' in the Hawaiian language. That sure sounds serene and quiet, but don't be too assured it won't ever erupt in the future.

A particularly mammoth sleeping volcano is **Mount Kilimanjaro** in Africa. It has a height of 5,895 m and comprises three volcanoes in all. But only one of them—the Kibo—is dormant, while the other two (Mawenzi and Shira) are extinct.

Though Europe doesn't have many volcanoes, there is a rather dangerous one called **Mount Teide** in Spain. It is a dormant volcano that hasn't erupted since 1909. However, if it explodes, it can become hazardous to the thousands of people who live nearby. Mount Teide is one of the sixteen 'Decade Volcanoes'. These sixteen volcanoes around the world are part of a United Nations project and is monitored extra closely by the International Association of Volcanology and Chemistry of the Earth's Interior (IAVCEI).

## EXERCISE 9: HIGHLIGHTS FROM YOUR VOLCANIC ADVENTURES

Are you sure you didn't get injured during your trip to some of the most dangerous volcanoes in the world? Look at the map and write down the names of the volcanoes corresponding to the labels 1–8. Alongside, write down the location of the volcano and state if it is active, dormant or extinct.

1. _____

2. _____

3. _____

4. _____

5. _____

6. _____

7. _____

8. _____

# WATERFALLS OF THE WORLD

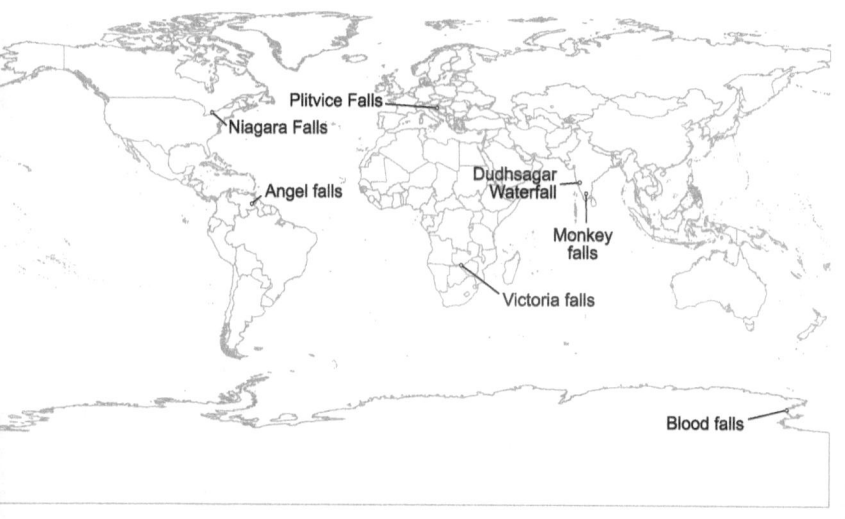

*Most famous waterfalls*

Have you ever bathed under a waterfall? Well, the shower in your bathroom is also a kind of waterfall! A **waterfall** occurs where a river or any other water body falls from a steep drop into a pool down below. Some waterfalls can be hundreds of m high, and you don't want to try and jump down with them!

A waterfall is formed due to a process called **erosion**. When a river flows, carrying sediment with it, it slowly erodes or breaks down the layer of rock under it. In due time, only hard rocks like granite remain. This granite forms cliffs and drops, and the river flows down them in the form of a waterfall. Sometimes waterfalls are also formed due to landslides, volcanoes, earthquakes and glaciers.

There are many types of waterfalls on Earth. Let us examine some of them.

**Block waterfall:** This falls down from a stream, such as the Niagara Falls in the US and Canada.

**Chute waterfall:** In this waterfall, the stream travels along a narrow passage at very high pressure. It will feel much stronger than your shower! The Three Chute Falls in Yosemite National Park, in the state of California, is a good example.

**Cascade waterfall:** If you were feeling disappointed that you cannot play about in a waterfall, then don't be. Cascade waterfalls are those that flow over a series of rocks that look exactly like steps on a staircase. Many of them, such as the Monkey Falls in Coimbatore in India, are perfectly safe for a good old water picnic.

**Fan waterfall**: As the waterfall descends, the water spreads out horizontally, resembling a fan! The Virgin Falls in Canada are among the prettiest water fans you'll find.

**Multi-step waterfalls:** These are a series of waterfalls where each step has its own pool. You can find a striking example in the Plitvice Lakes National Park in Croatia.

There are many other types of waterfalls in the world, such as **frozen waterfalls, punchbowl waterfalls** that have pools at their bases and **cataracts** that are especially powerful and dangerous.

No one knows exactly how many waterfalls there are on Earth, but let us go and visit some of the best ones. Are you ready with your waterproof gear?

## VICTORIA FALLS: THE EARTH'S LARGEST WATERFALL

The Victoria Falls isn't the tallest or the widest waterfall. And yet, this beautiful waterfall in Africa is considered the world's largest. Why? It's because no other waterfall produces this large a sheet of falling water! It is 1,708 m wide and 108 m high, and the water flows at the rate of 4,700 cubic metres per second—enough to leave you completely drenched!

The Victoria Falls is located on the border of Zambia and Zimbabwe. It is part of the Zambezi river that eventually leaves the falls and joins the Indian Ocean. Given the size of the fall, it might seem impossible to believe that you can swim in it. However, a rock wall has made a pool at the edge of the falls, rendering it safe for swimming. It is rightly called the 'Devil's Pool'!

Near the waterfall on the Zimbabwean side is the Victoria Falls rainforest. The constant water vapour that rises from the falls makes it rain here all the time, every single day. This famous spray or 'smoke' gave these falls their local name—Mosi-oa-Tunya—meaning 'The Smoke Which Thunders'.

## ANGEL FALLS: SO TALL, IT IS SCARY!

Imagine a tremendously forceful spray of water falling from a height of 979 m, uninterrupted and stopping for nothing. This waterfall is about three times as tall as the Eiffel Tower and only a few metres short of Mount Fuji in Japan. Feeling scared yet? The Angel Falls in Venezuela is the world's tallest waterfall and a spectacular sight!

These falls are located in the heart of the Canaima National Park and are a part of the Carrao river. The location of these falls is so remote that they were discovered only in 1933, by an American explorer named James Crawford Angel. The falls were eventually named after him.

The Angel Falls drop down from the Auyantepui mountain into a pool called the 'Devil's Canyon'. During the rainy season, the falls occasionally split into two. You can feel yourself getting sprayed with water even while standing a kilometre away!

## NIAGARA FALLS: THE CELEBRITY AMONG WATERFALLS

Possibly the most famous of all the waterfalls in the world is the Niagara Falls located on the border of the US and Canada. This stunning waterfall that has featured in hundreds of movies is actually not one, but three waterfalls rolled into one—the Horseshoe Falls, the American Falls and the Bridal Veil Falls. All three falls are part of the Niagara river and they combine to produce the celebrity! The tallest among these is the Horseshoe Falls, with a height of about 51 m. The water falls at the rate of 2,832 $m^3$/s.

If you see the water closely, you will find it looks greenish. The water comes from four 'Great Lakes'—Lake Superior, Lake Michigan, Lake Huron and Lake Erie. Continuous erosion creates a certain pulverized rock that looks blue-green due to its mineral content. This 'rock flour' is what imparts the green hue to the water.

The Niagara Falls is not only important to tourism but also to the generation of electricity. It is the fourth largest hydroelectric power plant in the US.

## BLOOD FALLS: A BLOOD-RED WATERFALL YOU WON'T BELIEVE IS REAL

Have you seen horror movies where blood (or tomato ketchup) is splattered everywhere? What would you say about a waterfall that oozes out blood? The Blood Falls in Antarctica emanates from the Taylor Glacier in one of Antarctica's dry valleys. The glacier is about 400 m tall, and the falls look exactly like blood escaping in great gushes, almost as if the Taylor Glacier is bleeding.

These waterfalls are among the most special in the world. What gives them a red colour? Oxidized iron! The water is highly saline and rich in iron. When this saline iron comes in contact with oxygen, it turns red. It is almost like the red rust you see on your instruments made of iron left out in the open.

Much like a wonder, microbes survive even in this water with high salt content, freezing temperature and massive amounts of iron.

Are there any other waterfalls on Earth with colourful water? The **Plitvice Falls** in Croatia has multi-coloured water where the colour changes depending on the season! The microbes in the water lend it a variety of colours from blue and green to grey.

## EXERCISE 10: HIGHLIGHTS FROM YOUR WATERFALL PICNICS

Did you bathe in some of the waterfalls you visited? Now that you're feeling fresh, study the maps and answer the questions.

1.

The waterfall you see on the map of Venezuela was closed to visitors until 1990. What is its name and why is it special?_____

2.

This waterfall falls over a series of rocks and is safe enough to bathe in. Can you name it and state its type?_____

3.

Can you name the waterfall in this map that is a major source of hydroelectricity? Also, name all the sources from where this waterfall gets its water. _____

4.

This gorgeous waterfall on the Zambezi river has an area called the 'Devil's Pool'. Can you make out from the map which waterfall it is? _____

5.

The waterfall in this map becomes truly stunning during the monsoon. Can you write down its name?_____

6.

What is the name of this waterfall with multi-coloured water in Croatia? _____

# LAKES OF THE WORLD

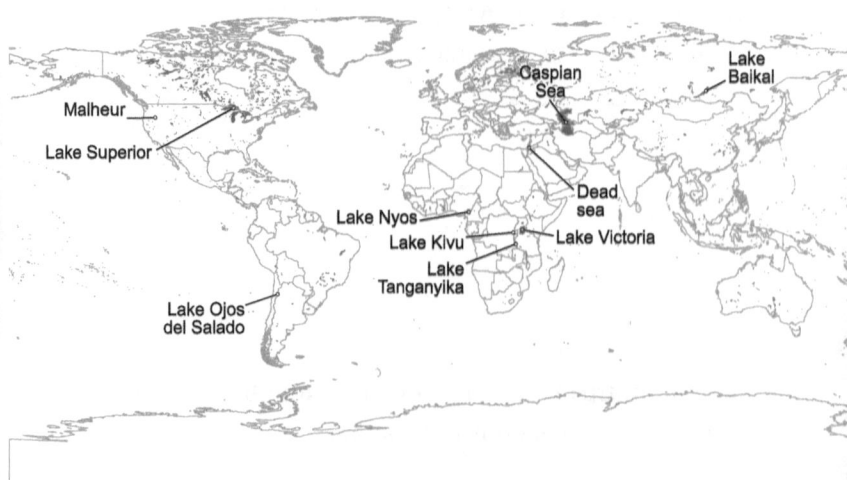

*Most famous lakes*

Have you ever sat at the lakeside, with a picnic basket in front of you and a favourite book in your hand? Lakes are wonderful treats of nature, to get you rejuvenated. But how is a lake different from a river? **Lakes** are water bodies that have land on all sides. They are much larger than ponds. Usually, lakes have freshwater; if the lake is clean enough, you can even drink the water straight out of it.

Like many geographical structures on Earth, lakes are also formed due to volcanoes, glacial activities or tectonic movement. Many large glaciers keep moving all the time, removing land and depositing ice-cold water in its place, in pits and depressions. These pits eventually turn into lakes.

Today, the '**Great Lakes**' or the five largest lakes in the world (Lake Superior, Lake Michigan, Lake Huron, Lake Erie and Lake Ontario) are in North America. Can you guess why? It is because many years ago the region was full of glaciers!

Geologists believe there are millions of lakes in the world. They are usually classified based on how they were formed. Some of the common types of lakes are:

**Fluvial lakes:** These are formed by rivers that bend from their usual course, like Carter Lake in the US.

**Glacial lakes:** The Great Lakes of North America are an example.

**Meteorite lakes:** These are formed by a meteor crash, like the Lonar Crater Lake in Maharashtra, India.

**Tectonic lakes:** These are like the Lake Baikal in Russia.

**Volcanic lakes:** The Malheur Lake in the US is an example.

Lakes may be called hard-working. They are home to thousands of plants, animals and fish. They are also useful to humans, especially to generate hydroelectricity (through dams). But tragically, many lakes are getting too polluted to be safe. This is happening because of human activity and the spread of pollution.

Let us travel to some of the largest and deepest lakes on Earth and unfold the secrets they keep within their waters.

## CASPIAN SEA: THE EARTH'S LARGEST LAKE

Wait, if this is a sea, how can it hold the record for being the world's largest lake? Well, the Caspian Sea, located between Europe and Asia, is technically a lake. It is the Earth's largest lake at 3,71,000 sq km! It is also quite deep; with its deepest part reaching 1,025 m. It was given the name 'Caspian Sea' by the ancient Romans, who, upon tasting the water, found that it was salty just like sea water. Bordering the Caspian Sea are the countries of Iran, Kazakhstan, Republic of Azerbaijan, Russia and Turkmenistan.

Most lakes have water sources that discharge water into them. Eventually, the lakes channel this water into basins. However, the Caspian Sea is a 'closed' lake. The Volga and the Ural in Russia discharge their water into the Caspian Sea. But the water does not go out anywhere except into the atmosphere through evaporation.

The Caspian Sea is very beneficial for all those who live near it. It is said to have resources of oil and natural gas. The sturgeon also lives here. Remember how you sampled caviar (made with surgeon eggs) on your trip to the Volga in Russia? But people have fished for sturgeon so much that their population is now under threat!

## LAKE BAIKAL: THE DEEPEST LAKE ON EARTH

If you want to go swimming, don't choose Lake Baikal in Siberia. It is the world's deepest lake at 1,620 m and freezes completely during winters! The shores abound in beautiful ice grottoes (or small ice caves). The bottom of the lake is full of 'mud' volcanoes. It spreads over a massive area of 31,722 sq km, making it the world's largest freshwater lake.

Most of the water of Lake Baikal comes from the Selenga river in Russia. The Angara river in Siberia takes the water out and discharges it into the Arctic Ocean. The fresh water here is among the purest in the world.

Lake Baikal is also one of the most beautiful and clear lakes you will ever see, thanks to the plankton that live in the water and feed on debris. Deep under the lake, the water is rich in oxygen—something that is rarely seen in any other lake.

Many fish and animals live in Lake Baikal, and many of them are endemic to it, which means that they are not found anywhere else. Look out for the nerpa—the world's only freshwater seal, and the omul—a fish that is a delicacy in the regions close to Lake Baikal. Can you guess how these fish survive in the winter when the lake freezes? The ice develops cracks that help oxygenate the water, letting the fish breathe.

## LAKE KIVU: DANGER ALERT!

Most people don't jump into the sea for a swim, but what harm could a quiet lake do? Lake Kivu located on the border of the Democratic Republic of Rwanda and Congo in Africa can *kill* you within minutes! This lethal lake spans an area of 2,700 sq km and flows out into the Ruzizi river in Africa.

So, what makes Lake Kivu so fatal? The water in this lake has about 65 km$^3$ of methane and 256 km$^3$ of carbon dioxide in it! Geologists claim that 40 per cent of the lake is now saturated with these two gases. More so, Lake Kivu is located near active volcanoes in Africa and if any of them explode, the lava can cause further problems. When the explosive gases reach the surface, there could be an explosion that could kill thousands of people!

### The Lake That Explodes

Are there more such dangerous lakes on Earth? **Lake Nyos** in Africa is a hazardous lake due to its carbon dioxide content. In 1986, the lake 'exploded', killing almost 1,700 people and also thousands of animals in the neighbouring village. The explosion led to carbon dioxide rising in concentration in the air.

## LAKE SUPERIOR: LARGEST LAKE IN NORTH AMERICA

Here is a lake that claims to be 'superior' even in its name! Lake Superior in North America is the largest of all the Great Lakes and covers a surface area of 82,170 sq km. It gets its water from over two hundred rivers—the Nipigon river and the Saint Louis river being prominent among them. The water eventually flows into the Saint Marys river to join Lake Huron, another Great Lake.

In 1648, a French missionary discovered the falls at Saint Marys and said that a 'superior lake' discharged the water into Lake Huron. And so, the name stuck! Although a major shipping hub today, the lake is prone to accidents because of fluctuating weather and depth.

The temperature of Lake Superior is congenial to life. The average temperature is around 4.4°C. This may seem cold, but the water in this lake rarely freezes over. Thank God for that, as aquatic creatures don't find ice as beautiful as we do!

Here, you will meet thousands of animals, fish (like carp and salmon), flowers, birds and diporeia. Diporeia are tiny shrimp-like creatures smaller than 10 mm. They are the favourite food of many fish that live in this lake.

## LAKE VICTORIA: AFRICA'S LARGEST LAKE

Lakes are supposed to be huge reservoirs of water, especially when you're referring to the largest lakes in a continent. But Lake Victoria, the largest lake in Africa, is reported to have dried up completely about 17,000 years ago due to a severe drought! However, today, it is a flourishing body of water stretching across 68,800 sq km in Kenya, Uganda and Tanzania. It is not deep for its size, going only as low as 84 m.

Since most of the water in Lake Victoria comes from direct rainfall, it is particularly prone to changes in weather. This lake's only outlet is the White Nile, one of the branches of the Nile river.

If you visit Lake Victoria, check out its beautiful archipelagos. Have the time of your life watching birds, monkeys and marine life on Ssese Islands, an archipelago comprising eighty-four islands. Sadly, Lake Victoria is struggling with the problem of pollution and over-fishing.

## EXERCISE 11: HIGHLIGHTS FROM YOUR LAKESIDE TOURS

How were your picnics by the most famous lakes in the world? It's time to recap your journey with some questions. Study the map and write down the names of the lakes corresponding to the labels 1–10.

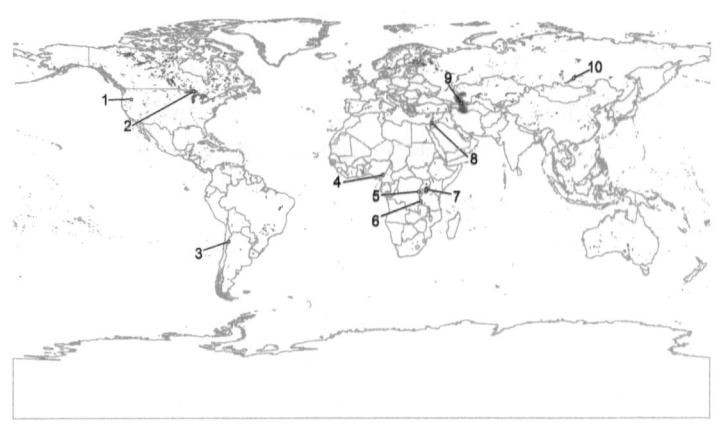

1. _____
2. _____
3. _____
4. _____
5. _____
6. _____
7. _____
8. _____
9. _____
10. _____

# ANSWERS

## EXERCISE 1: CONTINENTS OF THE WORLD

1.  Pangaea
2.  Europe
3.  North America
4.  Australia
5.  Africa
6.  South America
7.  Asia

## EXERCISE 2: COUNTRIES OF THE WORLD

1.  Germany
2.  Brazil
3.  Mexico
4.  Japan
5.  Fiji
6.  Chile
7.  South Africa
8.  New Zealand
9.  China, Asia
10. Nigeria
11. The UK
12. The US

## EXERCISE 3: OCEANS OF THE WORLD

1. Atlantic Ocean
2. Largest Ocean: Pacific Ocean
3. Southern Ocean
4. Indian Ocean
5. Smallest Ocean: Arctic Ocean

## EXERCISE 4: MOUNTAIN RANGES OF THE WORLD

1. Himalayas
2. Urals
3. Great Dividing Range
4. Eastern Ghats
5. Andes
6. Rockies
7. Karakoram
8. Mid-Atlantic Ridge
9. Alps
10. Pyrenees

## EXERCISE 5: RIVERS OF THE WORLD

1. Missouri, Mississipi
2. Amazon, Atlantic Ocean
3. Niger, Gulf of Guinea
4. Congo, Atlantic Ocean
5. Nile, Mediterranean Sea
6. Volga, Atlantic Ocean
7. Indus, Arabian Sea
8. Ganges, Sunderban Delta

9. Yangtse, China Sea

## EXERCISE 6: FORESTS OF THE WORLD

1. Amazon, South America
2. Congo Basin Forest, Africa
3. Sunderbans, Asia
4. Crooked Forest, Poland and Black Forest, Germany (Europe)
5. Tongass, North America
6. Taiga or Boreal | Europe, Asia, and North America

## EXERCISE 7: DESERTS OF THE WORLD

1. Mojave
2. Chihuahuan
3. Atacama
4. Sahara
5. Great Victoria
6. Gobi

## EXERCISE 8: ISLANDS OF THE WORLD

1. Tristan da Cunha, Atlantic
2. Bali, Sumatra, Borneo, Java
3. Greenland, Nuuk
4. Hunga Tonga, New Zealand
5. North Sentinel, India
6. Madagascar, Indian Ocean

## EXERCISE 9: VOLCANOES OF THE WORLD

1. Mount Vesuvius, Italy, Active
2. Mauna Loa, Hawaii, Active
3. Mount Merapi, Indonesia, Active
4. Mount Kilimanjaro, Africa, Dormant
5. Mount Kulal, Kenya, Extinct
6. Barren Island, India, Active
7. Mount Taal, Philippines, Active
8. Mount Fuji, Japan, Active

## EXERCISE 10: WATERFALLS OF THE WORLD

1. Angel Falls, Venezuela, the world's tallest waterfall
2. Monkey Falls, Coimbatore, India | Cascade waterfall
3. Niagara Falls | Sources: Lake Superior, Lake Michigan, Lake Huron and Lake Erie
4. Victoria Falls
5. Dudhsagar Falls, Goa, India
6. Plitvice Falls in Croatia

## EXERCISE 11: LAKES OF THE WORLD

1. Malheur Lake
2. Lake Superior
3. Lake Ojos del Salado
4. Lake Nyos
5. Lake Kivu
6. Lake Tanganyika
7. Lake Victoria
8. Dead Sea
9. Caspian Sea
10. Lake Baikal